A FAMILY AFFAIR
Maupassant Original Short Stories

Volume II

Guy de Maupassant

iBoo Press
London

A FAMILY AFFAIR
Maupassant Original Short Stories

Volume II

Guy de Maupassant

Layout & Cover © Copyright 2020 iBooPress, London

Published by
iBoo Press House

3rd Floor
86-90 Paul Street
London, EC2A4NE UK

t: +44 20 3695 0809
info@iboo.com II iBoo.com

ISBNs
978-1-64181-740-0 (p)

Printed in the United States

A FAMILY AFFAIR

Maupassant Original Short Stories

Volume II

Guy de Maupassant

Contents

THE COLONEL'S IDEAS

*U*pon my word," said Colonel Laporte, "although I am old and gouty, my legs as stiff as two pieces of wood, yet if a pretty woman were to tell me to go through the eye of a needle, I believe I should take a jump at it, like a clown through a hoop. I shall die like that; it is in the blood. I am an old beau, one of the old school, and the sight of a woman, a pretty woman, stirs me to the tips of my toes. There!

"We are all very much alike in France in this respect; we still remain knights, knights of love and fortune, since God has been abolished whose bodyguard we really were. But nobody can ever get woman out of our hearts; there she is, and there she will remain, and we love her, and shall continue to love her, and go on committing all kinds of follies on her account as long as there is a France on the map of Europe; and even if France were to be wiped off the map, there would always be Frenchmen left.

"When I am in the presence of a woman, of a pretty woman, I feel capable of anything. By Jove! when I feel her looks penetrating me, her confounded looks which set your blood on fire, I should like to do I don't know what; to fight a duel, to have a row, to smash the furniture, in order to show that I am the strongest, the bravest, the most daring and the most devoted of men.

"But I am not the only one, certainly not; the whole French army is like me, I swear to you. From the common soldier to the general, we all start out, from the van to the rear guard, when there is a woman in the case, a pretty woman. Do you remember what Joan of Arc made us do formerly? Come. I will make a bet that if a pretty woman had taken command of the army on the eve of Sedan, when Marshal MacMahon was wounded, we should have broken through the Prussian lines, by Jove! and had a drink out of their guns.

"It was not a Trochu, but a Sainte-Genevieve, who was needed in Paris; and I remember a little anecdote of the war which proves that we are capable of everything in presence of a woman.

"I was a captain, a simple captain, at the time, and I was in command of a detachment of scouts, who were retreating through a district which swarmed with Prussians. We were surrounded, pursued, tired out and half dead with fatigue and hunger, but we were bound to reach Bar-sur-Tain before the morrow, otherwise we should be shot, cut down, massacred. I do not know how we managed to escape so far. However, we had ten leagues to go during the night, ten leagues through the night, ten leagues through the snow, and with empty stomachs, and I thought to myself:

"'It is all over; my poor devils of fellows will never be able to do it.'

"We had eaten nothing since the day before, and the whole day long we remained hidden in a barn, huddled close together, so as not to feel the cold so much, unable to speak or even move, and sleeping by fits and starts, as one does when worn out with fatigue.

"It was dark by five o'clock, that wan darkness of the snow, and I shook my men. Some of them would not get up; they were almost incapable of moving or of standing upright; their joints were stiff from cold and hunger.

"Before us there was a large expanse of flat, bare country; the snow was still falling like a curtain, in large, white flakes, which concealed everything under a thick, frozen coverlet, a coverlet of frozen wool One might have thought that it was the end of the world.

"'Come, my lads, let us start.'

"They looked at the thick white flakes that were coming down, and they seemed to think: 'We have had enough of this; we may just as well die here!' Then I took out my revolver and said:

"'I will shoot the first man who flinches.' And so they set off, but very slowly, like men whose legs were of very little use to them, and I sent four of them three hundred yards ahead to scout, and the others followed pell-mell, walking at random and without any order. I put the strongest in the rear, with orders to quicken the pace of the sluggards with the points of their bayonets in the back.

"The snow seemed as if it were going to bury us alive; it powdered our kepis and cloaks without melting, and made phantoms of us, a kind of spectres of dead, weary soldiers. I said to myself: 'We shall never get out of this except by a miracle.'

"Sometimes we had to stop for a few minutes, on account of those who could not follow us, and then we heard nothing except the falling snow, that vague, almost undiscernible sound made by the falling flakes. Some of the men shook themselves, others did not move, and so I gave the order to set off again. They shouldered their rifles, and with weary feet we resumed our march, when suddenly the scouts fell back. Something had alarmed them; they had heard voices in front of them. I sent forward six men and a sergeant and waited.

"All at once a shrill cry, a woman's cry, pierced through the heavy silence of the snow, and in a few minutes they brought back two prisoners, an old man and a girl, whom I questioned in a low voice. They were escaping from the Prussians, who had occupied their house during the evening and had got drunk. The father was alarmed on his daughter's account, and, without even telling their servants, they had made their escape in the darkness. I saw immediately that they belonged to the better class. I invited them to accompany us, and we started off again, the old man who knew the road acting as our guide.

"It had ceased snowing, the stars appeared and the cold became intense. The girl, who was leaning on her father's arm, walked unsteadily as though in pain, and several times she murmured:

"'I have no feeling at all in my feet'; and I suffered more than she did to see that poor little woman dragging herself like that through the snow. But suddenly she stopped and said:

"'Father, I am so tired that I cannot go any further.'

"The old man wanted to carry her, but he could not even lift her up, and she sank to the ground with a deep sigh. We all gathered round her, and, as for me, I stamped my foot in perplexity, not knowing what to do, and being unwilling to abandon that man and girl like that, when suddenly one of the soldiers, a Parisian whom they had nicknamed Pratique, said:

"'Come, comrades, we must carry the young lady, otherwise we shall not show ourselves Frenchmen, confound it!'

"I really believe that I swore with pleasure. 'That is very good of you, my children,' I said; 'and I will take my share of the burden.'

"We could indistinctly see, through the darkness, the trees of a little wood on the left. Several of the men went into it, and soon came back with a bundle of branches made into a litter.

"'Who will lend his cape? It is for a pretty girl, comrades,' Pratique said, and ten cloaks were thrown to him. In a moment the girl was lying, warm and comfortable, among them, and was raised upon six shoulders. I placed myself at their head, on the right, well pleased with my position.

"We started off much more briskly, as if we had had a drink of wine, and I even heard some jokes. A woman is quite enough to electrify Frenchmen, you see. The soldiers, who had become cheerful and warm, had almost reformed their ranks, and an old 'franc-tireur' who was following the litter, waiting for his turn to replace the first of his comrades who might give out, said to one of his neighbors, loud enough for me to hear: "'I am not a young man now, but by—-, there is nothing like the women to put courage into you!'

"We went on, almost without stopping, until three o'clock in the morning, when suddenly our scouts fell back once more, and soon the whole detachment showed nothing but a vague shadow on the ground, as the men lay on the snow. I gave my orders in a low voice, and heard the harsh, metallic sound of the cocking, of rifles. For there, in the middle of the plain, some strange object was moving about. It looked like some enormous animal running about, now stretching out like a serpent, now coiling itself into a ball, darting to the right, then to the left, then stopping, and presently starting off again. But presently that wandering shape came nearer, and I saw a dozen lancers at full gallop, one behind the other. They had lost their way and were trying to find it.

"They were so near by that time that I could hear the loud breathing of their horses, the clinking of their swords and the creaking of their saddles, and cried: 'Fire!'

"Fifty rifle shots broke the stillness of the night, then there were four or five reports, and at last one single shot was heard, and when the smoke had cleared away, we saw that the twelve men and nine horses had fallen. Three of the animals were galloping away at a furious pace, and one of them was dragging the dead body of its rider, which rebounded violently from the ground; his foot had caught in the stirrup.

"One of the soldiers behind me gave a terrible laugh and said: 'There will be some widows there!'

"Perhaps he was married. A third added: 'It did not take long!'

"A head emerged from the litter.

"'What is the matter?' she asked; 'are you fighting?'

"'It is nothing, mademoiselle,' I replied; 'we have got rid of a dozen Prussians!'

"'Poor fellows!' she said. But as she was cold, she quickly disappeared beneath the cloaks again, and we started off once more. We marched on for a long time, and at last the sky began to grow lighter. The snow became quite clear, luminous and glistening, and a rosy tint appeared in the east. Suddenly a voice in the distance cried:

"'Who goes there?'

"The whole detachment halted, and I advanced to give the

countersign. We had reached the French lines, and, as my men defiled before the outpost, a commandant on horseback, whom I had informed of what had taken place, asked in a sonorous voice, as he saw the litter pass him: 'What have you in there?'

"And immediately a small head covered with light hair appeared, dishevelled and smiling, and replied:

"'It is I, monsieur.'

"At this the men raised a hearty laugh, and we felt quite light-hearted, while Pratique, who was walking by the side of the litter, waved his kepi and shouted:

"'Vive la France!' And I felt really affected. I do not know why, except that I thought it a pretty and gallant thing to say.

"It seemed to me as if we had just saved the whole of France and had done something that other men could not have done, something simple and really patriotic. I shall never forget that little face, you may be sure; and if I had to give my opinion about abolishing drums, trumpets and bugles, I should propose to replace them in every regiment by a pretty girl, and that would be even better than playing the 'Marseillaise: By Jove! it would put some spirit into a trooper to have a Madonna like that, a live Madonna, by the colonel's side."

He was silent for a few moments and then continued, with an air of conviction, and nodding his head:

"All the same, we are very fond of women, we Frenchmen!"

MOTHER SAUVAGE

Fifteen years had passed since I was at Virelogne. I returned there in the autumn to shoot with my friend Serval, who had at last rebuilt his chateau, which the Prussians had destroyed.

I loved that district. It is one of those delightful spots which have a sensuous charm for the eyes. You love it with a physical love. We, whom the country enchants, keep tender memories of certain springs, certain woods, certain pools, certain hills seen very often which have stirred us like joyful events. Sometimes our thoughts turn back to a corner in a forest, or the end of a bank, or an orchard filled with flowers, seen but a single time on some bright day, yet remaining in our hearts like the image of certain women met in the street on a spring morning in their light, gauzy dresses, leaving in soul and body an unsatisfied desire which is not to be forgotten, a feeling that you have just passed by happiness.

At Virelogne I loved the whole countryside, dotted with little woods and crossed by brooks which sparkled in the sun and looked like veins carrying blood to the earth. You fished in them for crawfish, trout and eels. Divine happiness! You could bathe in places and you often found snipe among the high grass which grew along the borders of these small water courses.

I was stepping along light as a goat, watching my two dogs running ahead of me, Serval, a hundred metres to my right, was beating a field of lucerne. I turned round by the thicket which forms the boundary of the wood of Sandres and I saw a cottage in ruins.

Suddenly I remembered it as I had seen it the last time, in 1869, neat, covered with vines, with chickens before the door. What is sadder than a dead house, with its skeleton standing bare and sinister?

I also recalled that inside its doors, after a very tiring day, the good woman had given me a glass of wine to drink and that Serval had told me the history of its people. The father, an old poacher, had been killed by the gendarmes. The son, whom I had once seen, was a tall, dry fellow who also passed for a fierce slayer of game. People called them "Les Sauvage."

Was that a name or a nickname?

I called to Serval. He came up with his long strides like a crane. I asked him:

"What's become of those people?"

This was his story:

When war was declared the son Sauvage, who was then thirty-three years old, enlisted, leaving his mother alone in the house. People did not pity the old woman very much because she had money; they knew it.

She remained entirely alone in that isolated dwelling, so far from the village, on the edge of the wood. She was not afraid, however, being of the same strain as the men folk—a hardy old woman, tall and thin, who seldom laughed and with whom one never jested. The women of the fields laugh but little in any case, that is men's business. But they themselves have sad and narrowed hearts, leading a melancholy, gloomy life. The peasants imbibe a little noisy merriment at the tavern, but their helpmates always have grave, stern countenances. The muscles of their faces have never learned the motions of laughter.

Mother Sauvage continued her ordinary existence in her cottage, which was soon covered by the snows. She came to the village once a week to get bread and a little meat. Then she returned to her house. As there was talk of wolves, she went out with a gun upon her shoulder—her son's gun, rusty and with the butt worn by the rubbing of the hand—and she was a strange sight, the tall "Sauvage," a little bent, going with slow strides over the snow, the muzzle of the piece extending beyond the black headdress, which confined her head and imprisoned her white hair, which no one had ever seen.

One day a Prussian force arrived. It was billeted upon the inhabitants, according to the property and resources of each. Four were allotted to the old woman, who was known to be rich.

They were four great fellows with fair complexion, blond beards and blue eyes, who had not grown thin in spite of the fatigue which they had endured already and who also, though in a conquered country, had remained kind and gentle. Alone with this aged woman, they showed themselves full of consideration, sparing her, as much as they could, all expense and fatigue. They could be seen, all four of them, making their toilet at the well in their shirt-sleeves in the gray dawn, splashing with great swishes of water their pink-white northern skin, while La Mere Sauvage went and came, preparing their soup. They would be seen cleaning the kitchen, rubbing the tiles, splitting wood, peeling potatoes, doing up all the housework like four good sons around their mother.

But the old woman thought always of her own son, so tall and thin, with his hooked nose and his brown eyes and his heavy mustache which made a roll of black hair upon his lip. She asked every day of each of the soldiers who were installed beside her hearth: "Do you know where the French marching regiment, No. 23, was sent? My boy is in it."

They invariably answered, "No, we don't know, don't know a thing at all." And, understanding her pain and her uneasiness— they who had mothers, too, there at home—they rendered her a thousand little services. She loved them well, moreover, her four enemies, since the peasantry have no patriotic hatred; that belongs to the upper class alone. The humble, those who pay the most because they are poor and because every new burden crushes them down; those who are killed in masses, who make the true cannon's prey because they are so many; those, in fine, who suffer most cruelly the atrocious miseries of war because they are the feeblest and offer least resistance—they hardly understand at all those bellicose ardors, that excitable sense of honor or those pretended political combinations which in six months exhaust two nations, the conqueror with the conquered.

They said in the district, in speaking of the Germans of La Mere Sauvage:

"There are four who have found a soft place."

Now, one morning, when the old woman was alone in the house, she observed, far off on the plain, a man coming toward her dwelling. Soon she recognized him; it was the postman to distribute the letters. He gave her a folded paper and she drew out of her case the spectacles which she used for sewing. Then she read:

MADAME SAUVAGE: This letter is to tell you sad news. Your boy Victor was killed yesterday by a shell which almost cut him in two. I was near by, as we stood next each other in the company, and he told me about you and asked me to let you know on the same day if anything happened to him.

I took his watch, which was in his pocket, to bring it back to you when the war is done.
CESAIRE RIVOT,

Soldier of the 2d class, March. Reg. No. 23.

The letter was dated three weeks back.

She did not cry at all. She remained motionless, so overcome and stupefied that she did not even suffer as yet. She thought: "There's Victor killed now." Then little by little the tears came to her eyes and the sorrow filled her heart. Her thoughts came, one by one, dreadful, torturing. She would never kiss him again, her child, her big boy, never again! The gendarmes had killed the father, the Prussians had killed the son. He had been cut in two by a cannon-ball. She seemed to see the thing, the horrible thing: the head falling, the eyes open, while he chewed the corner of his big mustache as he always did in moments of anger.

What had they done with his body afterward? If they had only let her have her boy back as they had brought back her husband— with the bullet in the middle of the forehead!

But she heard a noise of voices. It was the Prussians returning from the village. She hid her letter very quickly in her pocket, and she received them quietly, with her ordinary face, having had time to wipe her eyes.

They were laughing, all four, delighted, for they brought with them a fine rabbit—stolen, doubtless—and they made signs to the old woman that there was to be something good to east.

She set herself to work at once to prepare breakfast, but when it came to killing the rabbit, her heart failed her. And yet it was not the first. One of the soldiers struck it down with a blow of his fist behind the ears.

The beast once dead, she skinned the red body, but the sight of the blood which she was touching, and which covered her hands, and which she felt cooling and coagulating, made her tremble from head to foot, and she kept seeing her big boy cut in two, bloody, like this still palpitating animal.

She sat down at table with the Prussians, but she could not eat, not even a mouthful. They devoured the rabbit without bothering themselves about her. She looked at them sideways, without speaking, her face so impassive that they perceived nothing.

All of a sudden she said: "I don't even know your names, and here's a whole month that we've been together." They understood, not without difficulty, what she wanted, and told their names.

That was not sufficient; she had them written for her on a paper, with the addresses of their families, and, resting her spectacles on her great nose, she contemplated that strange handwriting, then folded the sheet and put it in her pocket, on top of the letter which told her of the death of her son.

When the meal was ended she said to the men:

"I am going to work for you."

And she began to carry up hay into the loft where they slept.

They were astonished at her taking all this trouble; she explained to them that thus they would not be so cold; and they helped her. They heaped the stacks of hay as high as the straw roof, and in that manner they made a sort of great chamber with four walls of fodder, warm and perfumed, where they should sleep splendidly.

At dinner one of them was worried to see that La Mere Sauvage still ate nothing. She told him that she had pains in her stomach. Then she kindled a good fire to warm herself, and the four Germans ascended to their lodging-place by the ladder which served them every night for this purpose.

As soon as they closed the trapdoor the old woman removed the ladder, then opened the outside door noiselessly and went back to look for more bundles of straw, with which she filled her kitchen. She went barefoot in the snow, so softly that no sound was heard. From time to time she listened to the sonorous and unequal snoring of the four soldiers who were fast asleep.

When she judged her preparations to be sufficient, she threw one of the bundles into the fireplace, and when it was alight she scattered it over all the others. Then she went outside again and looked.

In a few seconds the whole interior of the cottage was illumined with a brilliant light and became a frightful brasier, a gigantic fiery furnace, whose glare streamed out of the narrow window and threw a glittering beam upon the snow.

Then a great cry issued from the top of the house; it was a clamor of men shouting heartrending calls of anguish and of terror. Finally the trapdoor having given way, a whirlwind of fire shot up into the loft, pierced the straw roof, rose to the sky like the immense flame of a torch, and all the cottage flared.

Nothing more was heard therein but the crackling of the fire, the cracking of the walls, the falling of the rafters. Suddenly the roof fell in and the burning carcass of the dwelling hurled a great plume of sparks into the air, amid a cloud of smoke.

The country, all white, lit up by the fire, shone like a cloth of silver tinted with red.

A bell, far off, began to toll.

The old "Sauvage" stood before her ruined dwelling, armed with her gun, her son's gun, for fear one of those men might escape.

When she saw that it was ended, she threw her weapon into the brasier. A loud report followed.

People were coming, the peasants, the Prussians.

They found the woman seated on the trunk of a tree, calm and satisfied.

A German officer, but speaking French like a son of France, demanded:

"Where are your soldiers?"

She reached her bony arm toward the red heap of fire which was almost out and answered with a strong voice:

"There!"

They crowded round her. The Prussian asked:

"How did it take fire?"

"It was I who set it on fire."

They did not believe her, they thought that the sudden disaster had made her crazy. While all pressed round and listened, she told the story from beginning to end, from the arrival of the letter to the last shriek of the men who were burned with her house, and never omitted a detail.

When she had finished, she drew two pieces of paper from her pocket, and, in order to distinguish them by the last gleams of the fire, she again adjusted her spectacles. Then she said, showing one:

"That, that is the death of Victor." Showing the other, she added, indicating the red ruins with a bend of the head: "Here are their names, so that you can write home." She quietly held a sheet of paper out to the officer, who held her by the shoulders, and she continued:

"You must write how it happened, and you must say to their mothers that it was I who did that, Victoire Simon, la Sauvage! Do not forget."

The officer shouted some orders in German. They seized her, they threw her against the walls of her house, still hot. Then twelve men drew quickly up before her, at twenty paces. She did not move. She had understood; she waited.

An order rang out, followed instantly by a long report. A belated shot went off by itself, after the others.

The old woman did not fall. She sank as though they had cut off her legs.

The Prussian officer approached. She was almost cut in two, and in her withered hand she held her letter bathed with blood.

My friend Serval added:

"It was by way of reprisal that the Germans destroyed the chateau of the district, which belonged to me."

I thought of the mothers of those four fine fellows burned in that house and of the horrible heroism of that other mother shot against the wall.

And I picked up a little stone, still blackened by the flames.

EPIPHANY

I should say I did remember that Epiphany supper during the war! exclaimed Count de Garens, an army captain.

I was quartermaster of cavalry at the time, and for a fortnight had been scouting in front of the German advance guard. The evening before we had cut down a few Uhlans and had lost three men, one of whom was that poor little Raudeville. You remember Joseph de Raudeville, of course.

Well, on that day my commanding officer ordered me to take six troopers and to go and occupy the village of Porterin, where there had been five skirmishes in three weeks, and to hold it all night. There were not twenty houses left standing, not a dozen houses in that wasps' nest. So I took ten troopers and set out about four o'clock, and at five o'clock, while it was still pitch dark, we reached the first houses of Porterin. I halted and ordered Marchas—you know Pierre de Marchas, who afterward married little Martel-Auvelin, the daughter of the Marquis de Martel-Auvelin—to go alone into the village, and to report to me what he saw.

I had selected nothing but volunteers, all men of good family. It is pleasant when on duty not to be forced to be on intimate terms with unpleasant fellows. This Marchas was as smart as possible, cunning as a fox and supple as a serpent. He could scent the Prussians as a dog can scent a hare, could discover food where we should have died of hunger without him, and obtained information from everybody, and information which was always reliable, with incredible cleverness.

In ten minutes he returned. "All right," he said; "there have been no Prussians here for three days. It is a sinister place, is this village. I have been talking to a Sister of Mercy, who is caring for four or five wounded men in an abandoned convent."

I ordered them to ride on, and we entered the principal street. On the right and left we could vaguely see roofless walls, which were hardly visible in the profound darkness. Here and there a light was burning in a room; some family had remained to keep its house standing as well as they were able; a family of brave or of poor people. The rain began to fall, a fine, icy cold rain, which froze as it fell on our cloaks. The horses stumbled against stones, against beams, against furniture. Marchas guided us, going before us on foot, and leading his horse by the bridle.

"Where are you taking us to?" I asked him. And he replied: "I have a place for us to lodge in, and a rare good one." And we presently stopped before a small house, evidently belonging to some proprietor of the middle class. It stood on the street, was quite inclosed, and had a garden in the rear.

Marchas forced open the lock by means of a big stone which he picked up near the garden gate; then he mounted the steps, smashed in the front door with his feet and shoulders, lit a bit of wax candle, which he was never without, and went before us into the comfortable apartments of some rich private individual, guiding us with admirable assurance, as if he lived in this house which he now saw for the first time.

Two troopers remained outside to take care of our horses, and Marchas said to stout Ponderel, who followed him: "The stables must be on the left; I saw that as we came in; go and put the animals up there, for we do not need them"; and then, turning to me, he said: "Give your orders, confound it all!"

This fellow always astonished me, and I replied with a laugh: "I will post my sentinels at the country approaches and will return to you here."

"How many men are you going to take?"

"Five. The others will relieve them at five o'clock in the evening."

"Very well. Leave me four to look after provisions, to do the cooking and to set the table. I will go and find out where the wine is hidden."

I went off, to reconnoitre the deserted streets until they ended in the open country, so as to post my sentries there.

Half an hour later I was back, and found Marchas lounging in a great easy-chair, the covering of which he had taken off, from love of luxury, as he said. He was warming his feet at the fire and smoking an excellent cigar, whose perfume filled the room. He was alone, his elbows resting on the arms of the chair, his head sunk between his shoulders, his cheeks flushed, his eyes bright, and looking delighted.

I heard the noise of plates and dishes in the next room, and Marchas said * to me, smiling in a contented manner: "This is famous; I found the champagne under the flight of steps outside, the brandy—fifty bottles of the very finest in the kitchen garden under a pear tree, which did not seem to me to be quite straight when I looked at it by the light of my lantern. As for solids, we have two fowls, a goose, a duck, and three pigeons. They are being cooked at this moment. It is a delightful district."

I sat down opposite him, and the fire in the grate was burning my nose and cheeks. "Where did you find this wood?" I asked. "Splendid wood," he replied. "The owner's carriage. It is the paint which is causing all this flame, an essence of punch and varnish. A capital house!"

I laughed, for I saw the creature was funny, and he went on: "Fancy this being the Epiphany! I have had a bean put into the goose dressing; but there is no queen; it is really very annoying!" And I repeated like an echo: "It is annoying, but what do you want me to do in the matter?" "To find some, of course." "Some women. Women?—you must be mad?" "I managed to find the brandy under the pear tree, and the champagne under the steps; and yet there was nothing to guide me, while as for you, a petticoat is a sure bait. Go and look, old fellow."

He looked so grave, so convinced, that I could not tell whether he was joking or not, and so I replied: "Look here, Marchas, are you having a joke with me?" "I never joke on duty." "But where the devil do you expect me to find any women?" "Where you like; there must be two or three remaining in the neighborhood, so ferret them out and bring them here."

I got up, for it was too hot in front of the fire, and Marchas went off:

"Do you want an idea?" "Yes." "Go and see the priest." "The priest? What for?" "Ask him to supper, and beg him to bring a woman with him." "The priest! A woman! Ha! ha! ha!"

But Marchas continued with extraordinary gravity: "I am not laughing; go and find the priest and tell him how we are situated, and, as he must be horribly dull, he will come. But tell him that we want one woman at least, a lady, of course, since we, are all men of the world. He is sure to know his female parishioners on the tips of his fingers, and if there is one to suit us, and you manage it well, he will suggest her to you."

"Come, come, Marchas, what are you thinking of?" "My dear Garens, you can do this quite well. It will even be very funny. We are well bred, by Jove! and we will put on our most distinguished manners and our grandest style. Tell the abbe who we are, make him laugh, soften his heart, coax him and persuade him!" "No, it is impossible."

He drew his chair close to mine, and as he knew my special weakness, the scamp continued: "Just think what a swaggering thing it will be to do and how amusing to tell about; the whole army will talk about it, and it will give you a famous reputation."

I hesitated, for the adventure rather tempted me, and he persisted: "Come, my little Garens. You are the head of this detachment, and you alone can go and call on the head of the church in this neighborhood. I beg of you to go, and I promise you that after the war I will relate the whole affair in verse in the Revue de Deux Mondes. You owe this much to your men, for you have made them march enough during the last month."

I got up at last and asked: "Where is the priest's house?" "Take the second turning at the end of the street, you will see an avenue, and at the end of the avenue you will find the church. The parsonage is beside it." As I went out, he called out: "Tell him the bill of fare, to make him hungry!"

I discovered the ecclesiastic's little house without any difficulty; it was by the side of a large, ugly brick church. I knocked at the door with my fist, as there was neither bell nor knocker, and a loud voice from inside asked: "Who is there?" To which I replied: "A quartermaster of hussars."

I heard the noise of bolts and of a key being turned, and found myself face to face with a tall priest with a large stomach, the chest of a prizefighter, formidable hands projecting from turned-up sleeves, a red face, and the look of a kind man. I gave him a military salute and said: "Good-day, Monsieur le Cure."

He had feared a surprise, some marauders' ambush, and he smiled as he replied: "Good-day, my friend; come in." I followed him into a small room with a red tiled floor, in which a small fire was burning, very different to Marchas' furnace, and he gave me a chair and said: "What can I do for you?" "Monsieur, allow me first of all to introduce myself"; and I gave him my card, which he took and read half aloud: "Le Comte de Garens."

I continued: "There are eleven of us here, Monsieur l'Abbe, five on picket duty, and six installed at the house of an unknown inhabitant. The names of the six are: Garens, myself; Pierre de Marchas, Ludovic de Ponderel, Baron d'Streillis, Karl Massouligny, the painter's son, and Joseph Herbon, a young musician. I have come to ask you, in their name and my own, to do us the honor of supping with us. It is an Epiphany supper, Monsieur le Cure, and we should like to make it a little cheerful."

The priest smiled and murmured: "It seems to me to be hardly a suitable occasion for amusing one's self." And I replied: "We are fighting during the day, monsieur. Fourteen of our comrades have been killed in a month, and three fell as late as yesterday. It is war time. We stake our life at every moment; have we not, therefore, the right to amuse ourselves freely? We are Frenchmen, we like to laugh, and we can laugh everywhere. Our fathers laughed on the scaffold! This evening we should like to cheer ourselves up a little, like gentlemen, and not like soldiers; you understand me, I hope. Are we wrong?"

He replied quickly: "You are quite right, my friend, and I accept your invitation with great pleasure." Then he called out: "Hermance!"

An old bent, wrinkled, horrible peasant woman appeared and said: "What do you want?" "I shall not dine at home, my daughter." "Where are you going to dine then?" "With some gentlemen, the hussars."

I felt inclined to say: "Bring your servant with you," just to see Marchas' face, but I did not venture, and continued: "Do you know any one among your parishioners, male or female, whom I could invite as well?" He hesitated, reflected, and then said: "No, I do not know anybody!"

I persisted: "Nobody! Come, monsieur, think; it would be very nice to have some ladies, I mean to say, some married couples! I know nothing about your parishioners. The baker and his wife, the grocer, the—the—the—watchmaker—the—shoemaker— the—the druggist with Mrs. Druggist. We have a good spread and plenty of wine, and we should be enchanted to leave pleasant recollections of ourselves with the people here."

The priest thought again for a long time, and then said resolutely: "No, there is nobody." I began to laugh. "By Jove, Monsieur le Cure, it is very annoying not to have an Epiphany queen, for we have the bean. Come, think. Is there not a married mayor, or a married deputy mayor, or a married municipal councillor or a schoolmaster?" "No, all the ladies have gone away." "What, is there not in the whole place some good tradesman's wife with her good tradesman, to whom we might give this pleasure, for it would be a pleasure to them, a great pleasure under present circumstances?"

But, suddenly, the cure began to laugh, and laughed so violently that he fairly shook, and presently exclaimed: "Ha! ha! ha! I have got what you want, yes. I have got what you want! Ha! ha! ha! We will laugh and enjoy ourselves, my children; we will have some fun. How pleased the ladies will be, I say, how delighted they will be! Ha! ha! Where are you staying?"

I described the house, and he understood where it was. "Very good," he said. "It belongs to Monsieur Bertin-Lavaille. I will be there in half an hour, with four ladies! Ha! ha! ha! four ladies!"

He went out with me, still laughing, and left me, repeating: "That is capital; in half an hour at Bertin-Lavaille's house."

I returned quickly, very much astonished and very much puzzled. "Covers for how many?" Marchas asked, as soon as he saw me. "Eleven. There are six of us hussars, besides the priest and four ladies." He was thunderstruck, and I was triumphant. He repeated: "Four ladies! Did you say, four ladies?" "I said four women." "Real women?" "Real women." "Well, accept my compliments!" "I will, for I deserve them."

He got out of his armchair, opened the door, and I saw a beautiful white tablecloth on a long table, round which three hussars in blue aprons were setting out the plates and glasses. "There are some women coming!" Marchas cried. And the three men began to dance and to cheer with all their might.

Everything was ready, and we were waiting. We waited for nearly an hour, while a delicious smell of roast poultry pervaded the whole house. At last, however, a knock against the shutters made us all jump up at the same moment. Stout Ponderel ran to open the door, and in less than a minute a little Sister of Mercy appeared in the doorway. She was thin, wrinkled and timid, and successively greeted the four bewildered hussars who saw her enter. Behind her, the noise of sticks sounded on the tiled floor in the vestibule, and as soon as she had come into the drawing-room, I saw three old heads in white caps, following each other one by one, who came in, swaying with different movements, one inclining to the right, while the other inclined to the left. And three worthy women appeared, limping, dragging their legs behind them, crippled by illness and deformed through old age, three infirm old women, past service, the only three pensioners who were able to walk in the home presided over by Sister Saint-Benedict.

She had turned round to her invalids, full of anxiety for them, and then, seeing my quartermaster's stripes, she said to me: "I am much obliged to you for thinking of these poor women. They have very little pleasure in life, and you are at the same time giving them a great treat and doing them a great honor."

I saw the priest, who had remained in the dark hallway, and was laughing heartily, and I began to laugh in my turn, especially when I saw Marchas' face. Then, motioning the nun to the seats, I said:

"Sit down, sister; we are very proud and very happy that you have accepted our unpretentious invitation."

She took three chairs which stood against the wall, set them before the fire, led her three old women to them, settled them on them, took their sticks and shawls, which she put into a corner, and then, pointing to the first, a thin woman with an enormous stomach, who was evidently suffering from the dropsy, she said: "This is Mother Paumelle; whose husband was killed by falling from a roof, and whose son died in Africa; she is sixty years old." Then she pointed to another, a tall woman, whose head trembled unceasingly: "This is Mother Jean-Jean, who is sixty-seven. She is nearly blind, for her face was terribly singed in a fire, and her right leg was half burned off."

Then she pointed to the third, a sort of dwarf, with protruding, round, stupid eyes, which she rolled incessantly in all directions, "This is La Putois, an idiot. She is only forty-four."

I bowed to the three women as if I were being presented to some royal highnesses, and turning to the priest, I said: "You are an excellent man, Monsieur l'Abbe, to whom all of us here owe a debt of gratitude."

Everybody was laughing, in fact, except Marchas, who seemed furious, and just then Karl Massouligny cried: "Sister Saint-Benedict, supper is on the table!"

I made her go first with the priest, then I helped up Mother Paumelle, whose arm I took and dragged her into the next room, which was no easy task, for she seemed heavier than a lump of iron.

Stout Ponderel gave his arm to Mother Jean-Jean, who bemoaned her crutch, and little Joseph Herbon took the idiot, La Putois, to the dining-room, which was filled with the odor of the viands.

As soon as we were opposite our plates, the sister clapped her hands three times, and, with the precision of soldiers presenting arms, the women made a rapid sign of the cross, and then the priest slowly repeated the Benedictus in Latin. Then we sat down, and the two fowls appeared, brought in by Marchas, who chose to wait at table, rather than to sit down as a guest to this ridiculous repast.

But I cried: "Bring the champagne at once!" and a cork flew out with the noise of a pistol, and in spite of the resistance of the priest and of the kind sister, the three hussars, sitting by the side of the three invalids, emptied their three full glasses down their throats by force.

Massouligny, who possessed the faculty of making himself at home, and of being on good terms with every one, wherever he was, made love to Mother Paumelle in the drollest manner. The dropsical woman, who had retained her cheerfulness in spite of her misfortunes, answered him banteringly in a high falsetto voice which appeared as if it were put on, and she laughed so heartily at her neighbor's jokes that it was quite alarming. Little Herbon had seriously undertaken the task of making the idiot drunk, and Baron d'Streillis, whose wits were not always particularly sharp, was questioning old Jean-Jean about the life, the habits, and the rules of the hospital.

The nun said to Massouligny in consternation:

"Oh! oh! you will make her ill; pray do not make her laugh like that, monsieur. Oh! monsieur—" Then she got up and rushed at Herbon to take from him a full glass which he was hastily emptying down La Putois' throat, while the priest shook with laughter, and said to the sister: "Never mind; just this once, it will not hurt them. Do leave them alone."

After the two fowls they ate the duck, which was flanked by the three pigeons and the blackbird, and then the goose appeared, smoking, golden-brown, and diffusing a warm odor of hot, browned roast meat. La Paumelle, who was getting lively, clapped her hands; La Jean-Jean left off answering the baron's numerous questions, and La Putois uttered grunts of pleasure, half cries and half sighs, as little children do when one shows them candy. "Allow me to take charge of this animal," the cure said. "I understand these sort of operations better than most people." "Certainly, Monsieur l'Abbe," and the sister said: "How would it be to open the window a little? They are too warm, and I am afraid they will be ill."

I turned to Marchas: "Open the window for a minute." He did so; the cold outer air as it came in made the candles flare, and the steam from the goose, which the cure was scientifically carving, with a table napkin round his neck, whirl about. We watched him doing it, without speaking now, for we were interested in his attractive handiwork, and seized with renewed appetite at the sight of that enormous golden-brown bird, whose limbs fell one after another into the brown gravy at the bottom of the dish. At that moment, in the midst of that greedy silence which kept us all attentive, the distant report of a shot came in at the open window.

I started to my feet so quickly that my chair fell down behind me, and I shouted: "To saddle, all of you! You, Marchas, take two men and go and see what it is. I shall expect you back here in five minutes." And while the three riders went off at full gallop through the night, I got into the saddle with my three remaining hussars, in front of the steps of the villa, while the cure, the sister and the three old women showed their frightened faces at the window.

We heard nothing more, except the barking of a dog in the distance. The rain had ceased, and it was cold, very cold, and soon I heard the gallop of a horse, of a single horse, coming back. It was Marchas, and I called out to him: "Well?" "It is nothing; Francois has wounded an old peasant who refused to answer his challenge: 'Who goes there?' and who continued to advance in spite of the order to keep off; but they are bringing him here, and we shall see what is the matter."

I gave orders for the horses to be put back in the stable, and I sent my two soldiers to meet the others, and returned to the house. Then the cure, Marchas, and I took a mattress into the room to lay the wounded man on; the sister tore up a table napkin in order to make lint, while the three frightened women remained huddled up in a corner.

Soon I heard the rattle of sabres on the road, and I took a candle to show a light to the men who were returning; and they soon appeared, carrying that inert, soft, long, sinister object which a human body becomes when life no longer sustains it.

They put the wounded man on the mattress that had been prepared for him, and I saw at the first glance that he was dying. He had the death rattle and was spitting up blood, which ran out of the corners of his mouth at every gasp. The man was covered with blood! His cheeks, his beard, his hair, his neck and his clothes seemed to have been soaked, to have been dipped in a red tub; and that blood stuck to him, and had become a dull color which was horrible to look at.

The wounded man, wrapped up in a large shepherd's cloak, occasionally opened his dull, vacant eyes, which seemed stupid with astonishment, like those of animals wounded by a sportsman, which fall at his feet, more than half dead already, stupefied with terror and surprise.

The cure exclaimed: "Ah, it is old Placide, the shepherd from Les Moulins. He is deaf, poor man, and heard nothing. Ah! Oh, God! they have killed the unhappy man!" The sister had opened his blouse and shirt, and was looking at a little blue hole in his chest, which was not bleeding any more. "There is nothing to be done," she said.

The shepherd was gasping terribly and bringing up blood with every last breath, and in his throat, to the very depth of his lungs, they could hear an ominous and continued gurgling. The cure, standing in front of him, raised his right hand, made the sign of the cross, and in a slow and solemn voice pronounced the Latin words which purify men's souls, but before they were finished, the old man's body trembled violently, as if something had given way inside him, and he ceased to breathe. He was dead.

When I turned round, I saw a sight which was even more horrible than the death struggle of this unfortunate man; the three old women were standing up huddled close together, hideous, and grimacing with fear and horror. I went up to them, and they began to utter shrill screams, while La Jean-Jean, whose burned leg could no longer support her, fell to the ground at full length.

Sister Saint-Benedict left the dead man, ran up to her infirm old women, and without a word or a look for me, wrapped their shawls round them, gave them their crutches, pushed them to the door, made them go out, and disappeared with them into the dark night.

I saw that I could not even let a hussar accompany them, for the mere rattle of a sword would have sent them mad with fear.

The cure was still looking at the dead man; but at last he turned round to me and said:

"Oh! What a horrible thing!"

THE MUSTACHE

CHATEAU DE SOLLES,
July 30, 1883.

*M*y Dear Lucy:
I have no news. We live in the drawing-room, looking out at the rain. We cannot go out in this frightful weather, so we have theatricals. How stupid they are, my dear, these drawing entertainments in the repertory of real life! All is forced, coarse, heavy. The jokes are like cannon balls, smashing everything in their passage. No wit, nothing natural, no sprightliness, no elegance. These literary men, in truth, know nothing of society. They are perfectly ignorant of how people think and talk in our set. I do not mind if they despise our customs, our conventionalities, but I do not forgive them for not knowing them. When they want to be humorous they make puns that would do for a barrack; when they try to be jolly, they give us jokes that they must have picked up on the outer boulevard in those beer houses artists are supposed to frequent, where one has heard the same students' jokes for fifty years.

So we have taken to Theatricals. As we are only two women, my husband takes the part of a soubrette, and, in order to do that, he has shaved off his mustache. You cannot imagine, my dear Lucy, how it changes him! I no longer recognize him-by day or at night. If he did not let it grow again I think I should no longer love him; he looks so horrid like this.

In fact, a man without a mustache is no longer a man. I do not care much for a beard; it almost always makes a man look untidy. But a mustache, oh, a mustache is indispensable to a manly face. No, you would never believe how these little hair bristles on the upper lip are a relief to the eye and good in other ways. I have thought over the matter a great deal but hardly dare to write my thoughts. Words look so different on paper and the subject is so difficult, so delicate, so dangerous that it requires infinite skill to tackle it.

Well, when my husband appeared, shaven, I understood at once that I never could fall in love with a strolling actor nor a preacher, even if it were Father Didon, the most charming of all! Later when I was alone with him (my husband) it was worse still. Oh, my dear Lucy, never let yourself be kissed by a man without a mustache; their kisses have no flavor, none whatever! They no longer have the charm, the mellowness and the snap —yes, the snap—of a real kiss. The mustache is the spice.

Imagine placing to your lips a piece of dry—or moist—parchment. That is the kiss of the man without a mustache. It is not worth while.

Whence comes this charm of the mustache, will you tell me? Do I know myself? It tickles your face, you feel it approaching your mouth and it sends a little shiver through you down to the tips of your toes.

And on your neck! Have you ever felt a mustache on your neck? It intoxicates you, makes you feel creepy, goes to the tips of your fingers. You wriggle, shake your shoulders, toss back your head. You wish to get away and at the same time to remain there; it is delightful, but irritating. But how good it is!

A lip without a mustache is like a body without clothing; and one must wear clothes, very few, if you like, but still some clothing.

I recall a sentence (uttered by a politician) which has been running in my mind for three months. My husband, who keeps up with the newspapers, read me one evening a very singular speech by our Minister of Agriculture, who was called M. Meline. He may have been superseded by this time. I do not know.

I was paying no attention, but the name Meline struck me. It recalled, I do not exactly know why, the 'Scenes de la vie de boheme'. I thought it was about some grisette. That shows how scraps of the speech entered my mind. This M. Meline was making this statement to the people of Amiens, I believe, and I have ever since been trying to understand what he meant: "There is no patriotism without agriculture!" Well, I have just discovered his meaning, and I affirm in my turn that there is no love without a mustache. When you say it that way it sounds comical, does it not?

There is no love without a mustache!

"There is no patriotism without agriculture," said M. Meline, and he was right, that minister; I now understand why.

From a very different point of view the mustache is essential. It gives character to the face. It makes a man look gentle, tender, violent, a monster, a rake, enterprising! The hairy man, who does not shave off his whiskers, never has a refined look, for his features are concealed; and the shape of the jaw and the chin betrays a great deal to those who understand.

The man with a mustache retains his own peculiar expression and his refinement at the same time.

And how many different varieties of mustaches there are! Sometimes they are twisted, curled, coquettish. Those seem to be chiefly devoted to women.

Sometimes they are pointed, sharp as needles, and threatening. That kind prefers wine, horses and war.

Sometimes they are enormous, overhanging, frightful. These big ones generally conceal a fine disposition, a kindliness that borders on weakness and a gentleness that savors of timidity.

But what I adore above all in the mustache is that it is French, altogether French. It came from our ancestors, the Gauls, and has remained the insignia of our national character.

It is boastful, gallant and brave. It sips wine gracefully and knows how to laugh with refinement, while the broad-bearded jaws are clumsy in everything they do.

I recall something that made me weep all my tears and also—I see it now—made me love a mustache on a man's face.

It was during the war, when I was living with my father. I was a young girl then. One day there was a skirmish near the chateau. I had heard the firing of the cannon and of the artillery all the morning, and that evening a German colonel came and took up his abode in our house. He left the following day.

My father was informed that there were a number of dead bodies in the fields. He had them brought to our place so that they might be buried together. They were laid all along the great avenue of pines as fast as they brought them in, on both sides of the avenue, and as they began to smell unpleasant, their bodies were covered with earth until the deep trench could be dug. Thus one saw only their heads which seemed to protrude from the clayey earth and were almost as yellow, with their closed eyes.

I wanted to see them. But when I saw those two rows of frightful faces, I thought I should faint. However, I began to look at them, one by one, trying to guess what kind of men these had been.

The uniforms were concealed beneath the earth, and yet immediately, yes, immediately, my dear, I recognized the Frenchmen by their mustache!

Some of them had shaved on the very day of the battle, as though they wished to be elegant up to the last; others seemed to have a week's growth, but all wore the French mustache, very plain, the proud mustache that seems to say: "Do not take me for my bearded friend, little one; I am a brother."

And I cried, oh, I cried a great deal more than I should if I had not recognized them, the poor dead fellows.

It was wrong of me to tell you this. Now I am sad and cannot chatter any

longer. Well, good-by, dear Lucy. I send you a hearty kiss. Long live

the mustache!

JEANNE.

MADAME BAPTISTE

The first thing I did was to look at the clock as I entered the waiting-room of the station at Loubain, and I found that I had to wait two hours and ten minutes for the Paris express.

I had walked twenty miles and felt suddenly tired. Not seeing anything on the station walls to amuse me, I went outside and stood there racking my brains to think of something to do. The street was a kind of boulevard, planted with acacias, and on either side a row of houses of varying shape and different styles of architecture, houses such as one only sees in a small town, and ascended a slight hill, at the extreme end of which there were some trees, as though it ended in a park.

From time to time a cat crossed the street and jumped over the gutters carefully. A cur sniffed at every tree and hunted for scraps from the kitchens, but I did not see a single human being, and I felt listless and disheartened. What could I do with myself? I was already thinking of the inevitable and interminable visit to the small cafe at the railway station, where I should have to sit over a glass of undrinkable beer and the illegible newspaper, when I saw a funeral procession coming out of a side street into the one in which I was, and the sight of the hearse was a relief to me. It would, at any rate, give me something to do for ten minutes.

Suddenly, however, my curiosity was aroused. The hearse was followed by eight gentlemen, one of whom was weeping, while the others were chatting together, but there was no priest, and I thought to myself:

"This is a non-religious funeral," and then I reflected that a town like Loubain must contain at least a hundred freethinkers, who would have made a point of making a manifestation. What could it be, then? The rapid pace of the procession clearly proved that the body was to be buried without ceremony, and, consequently, without the intervention of the Church.

My idle curiosity framed the most complicated surmises, and as the hearse passed me, a strange idea struck me, which was to follow it, with the eight gentlemen. That would take up my time for an hour, at least, and I accordingly walked with the others, with a sad look on my face, and, on seeing this, the two last turned round in surprise, and then spoke to each other in a low voice.

No doubt they were asking each other whether I belonged to the town, and then they consulted the two in front of them, who stared at me in turn. This close scrutiny annoyed me, and to put an end to it I went up to them, and, after bowing, I said:

"I beg your pardon, gentlemen, for interrupting your conversation, but, seeing a civil funeral, I have followed it, although I did not know the deceased gentleman whom you are accompanying."

"It was a woman," one of them said.

I was much surprised at hearing this, and asked:

"But it is a civil funeral, is it not?"

The other gentleman, who evidently wished to tell me all about it, then said: "Yes and no. The clergy have refused to allow us the use of the church."

On hearing this I uttered a prolonged "A-h!" of astonishment. I could not understand it at all, but my obliging neighbor continued:

"It is rather a long story. This young woman committed suicide, and that is the reason why she cannot be buried with any religious ceremony. The gentleman who is walking first, and who is crying, is her husband."

I replied with some hesitation:

"You surprise and interest me very much, monsieur. Shall I be indiscreet if I ask you to tell me the facts of the case? If I am troubling you, forget that I have said anything about the matter."

The gentleman took my arm familiarly.

"Not at all, not at all. Let us linger a little behind the others, and I will tell it you, although it is a very sad story. We have plenty of time before getting to the cemetery, the trees of which you see up yonder, for it is a stiff pull up this hill."

And he began:

"This young woman, Madame Paul Hamot, was the daughter of a wealthy merchant in the neighborhood, Monsieur Fontanelle. When she was a mere child of eleven, she had a shocking adventure; a footman attacked her and she nearly died. A terrible criminal case was the result, and the man was sentenced to penal servitude for life.

"The little girl grew up, stigmatized by disgrace, isolated, without any companions; and grown-up people would scarcely kiss her, for they thought that they would soil their lips if they touched her forehead, and she became a sort of monster, a phenomenon to all the town. People said to each other in a whisper: 'You know, little Fontanelle,' and everybody turned away in the streets when she passed. Her parents could not even get a nurse to take her out for a walk, as the other servants held aloof from her, as if contact with her would poison everybody who came near her.

"It was pitiable to see the poor child go and play every afternoon. She remained quite by herself, standing by her maid and looking at the other children amusing themselves. Sometimes, yielding to an irresistible desire to mix with the other children, she advanced timidly, with nervous gestures, and mingled with a group, with furtive steps, as if conscious of her own disgrace. And immediately the mothers, aunts and nurses would come running from every seat and take the children entrusted to their care by the hand and drag them brutally away.

"Little Fontanelle remained isolated, wretched, without understanding what it meant, and then she began to cry, nearly heartbroken with grief, and then she used to run and hide her head in her nurse's lap, sobbing.

"As she grew up, it was worse still. They kept the girls from her, as if she were stricken with the plague. Remember that she had nothing to learn, nothing; that she no longer had the right to the symbolical wreath of orange-flowers; that almost before she could read she had penetrated that redoubtable mystery which mothers scarcely allow their daughters to guess at, trembling as they enlighten them on the night of their marriage.

"When she went through the streets, always accompanied by her governess, as if, her parents feared some fresh, terrible adventure, with her eyes cast down under the load of that mysterious disgrace which she felt was always weighing upon her, the other girls, who were not nearly so innocent as people thought, whispered and giggled as they looked at her knowingly, and immediately turned their heads absently, if she happened to look at them. People scarcely greeted her; only a few men bowed to her, and the mothers pretended not to see her, while some young blackguards called her Madame Baptiste, after the name of the footman who had attacked her.

"Nobody knew the secret torture of her mind, for she hardly ever spoke, and never laughed, and her parents themselves appeared uncomfortable in her presence, as if they bore her a constant grudge for some irreparable fault.

"An honest man would not willingly give his hand to a liberated convict, would he, even if that convict were his own son?

And Monsieur and Madame Fontanelle looked on their daughter as they would have done on a son who had just been released from the hulks. She was pretty and pale, tall, slender, distinguished-looking, and she would have pleased me very much, monsieur, but for that unfortunate affair.

"Well, when a new sub-prefect was appointed here, eighteen months ago, he brought his private secretary with him. He was a queer sort of fellow, who had lived in the Latin Quarter, it appears. He saw Mademoiselle Fontanelle and fell in love with her, and when told of what occurred, he merely said:

"'Bah! That is just a guarantee for the future, and I would rather it should have happened before I married her than afterward. I shall live tranquilly with that woman.'

"He paid his addresses to her, asked for her hand and married her, and then, not being deficient in assurance, he paid wedding calls, as if nothing had happened. Some people returned them, others did not; but, at last, the affair began to be forgotten, and she took her proper place in society.

"She adored her husband as if he had been a god; for, you must remember, he had restored her to honor and to social life, had braved public opinion, faced insults, and, in a word, performed such a courageous act as few men would undertake, and she felt the most exalted and tender love for him.

"When she became enceinte, and it was known, the most particular people and the greatest sticklers opened their doors to her, as if she had been definitely purified by maternity.

"It is strange, but so it is, and thus everything was going on as well as possible until the other day, which was the feast of the patron saint of our town. The prefect, surrounded by his staff and the authorities, presided at the musical competition, and when he had finished his speech the distribution of medals began, which Paul Hamot, his private secretary, handed to those who were entitled to them.

"As you know, there are always jealousies and rivalries, which make people forget all propriety. All the ladies of the town were there on the platform, and, in his turn, the bandmaster from the village of Mourmillon came up. This band was only to receive a second-class medal, for one cannot give first-class medals to everybody, can one? But when the private secretary handed him his badge, the man threw it in his face and exclaimed:

"'You may keep your medal for Baptiste. You owe him a first-class one, also, just as you do me.'

"There were a number of people there who began to laugh. The common herd are neither charitable nor refined, and every eye was turned toward that poor lady. Have you ever seen a woman going mad, monsieur? Well, we were present at the sight! She got up and fell back on her chair three times in succession, as if she wished to make her escape, but saw that she could not make her way through the crowd, and then another voice in the crowd exclaimed:

"'Oh! Oh! Madame Baptiste!'

"And a great uproar, partly of laughter and partly of indignation, arose. The word was repeated over and over again; people stood on tiptoe to see the unhappy woman's face; husbands lifted their wives up in their arms, so that they might see her, and people asked:

"'Which is she? The one in blue?'

"The boys crowed like cocks, and laughter was heard all over the place.

"She did not move now on her state chair, but sat just as if she had been put there for the crowd to look at. She could not move, nor conceal herself, nor hide her face. Her eyelids blinked quickly, as if a vivid light were shining on them, and she breathed heavily, like a horse that is going up a steep hill, so that it almost broke one's heart to see her. Meanwhile, however, Monsieur Hamot had seized the ruffian by the throat, and they were rolling on the ground together, amid a scene of indescribable confusion, and the ceremony was interrupted.

"An hour later, as the Hamots were returning home, the young woman, who had not uttered a word since the insult, but who was trembling as if all her nerves had been set in motion by springs, suddenly sprang over the parapet of the bridge and threw herself into the river before her husband could prevent her. The water is very deep under the arches, and it was two hours before her body was recovered. Of course, she was dead."

The narrator stopped and then added:

"It was, perhaps, the best thing she could do under the circumstances. There are some things which cannot be wiped out, and now you understand why the clergy refused to have her taken into church. Ah! If it had been a religious funeral the whole town would have been present, but you can understand that her suicide added to the other affair and made families abstain from attending her funeral; and then, it is not an easy matter here to attend a funeral which is performed without religious rites."

We passed through the cemetery gates and I waited, much moved by what I had heard, until the coffin had been lowered into the grave, before I went up to the poor fellow who was sobbing violently, to press his hand warmly. He looked at me in surprise through his tears and then said:

"Thank you, monsieur." And I was not sorry that I had followed the funeral.

THE QUESTION OF LATIN

*T*his subject of Latin that has been dinned into our ears for some time past recalls to my mind a story—a story of my youth.

I was finishing my studies with a teacher, in a big central town, at the Institution Robineau, celebrated through the entire province for the special attention paid there to the study of Latin.

For the past ten years, the Robineau Institute beat the imperial lycee of the town at every competitive examination, and all the colleges of the subprefecture, and these constant successes were due, they said, to an usher, a simple usher, M. Piquedent, or rather Pere Piquedent.

He was one of those middle-aged men quite gray, whose real age it is impossible to tell, and whose history we can guess at first glance. Having entered as an usher at twenty into the first institution that presented itself so that he could proceed to take first his degree of Master of Arts and afterward the degree of Doctor of Laws, he found himself so enmeshed in this routine that he remained an usher all his life. But his love for Latin did not leave him and harassed him like an unhealthy passion. He continued to read the poets, the prose writers, the historians, to interpret them and penetrate their meaning, to comment on them with a perseverance bordering on madness.

One day, the idea came into his head to oblige all the students in his class to answer him in Latin only; and he persisted in this resolution until at last they were capable of sustaining an entire conversation with him just as they would in their mother tongue. He listened to them, as a leader of an orchestra listens to his musicians rehearsing, and striking his desk every moment with his ruler, he exclaimed:

"Monsieur Lefrere, Monsieur Lefrere, you are committing a solecism! You forget the rule.

"Monsieur Plantel, your way of expressing yourself is altogether French and in no way Latin. You must understand the genius of a language. Look here, listen to me."

Now, it came to pass that the pupils of the Institution Robineau carried off, at the end of the year, all the prizes for composition, translation, and Latin conversation.

Next year, the principal, a little man, as cunning as an ape, whom he resembled in his grinning and grotesque appearance, had had printed on his programmes, on his advertisements, and painted on the door of his institution:

"Latin Studies a Specialty. Five first prizes carried off in the five classes of the lycee.

"Two honor prizes at the general examinations in competition with all the lycees and colleges of France."

For ten years the Institution Robineau triumphed in the same fashion. Now my father, allured by these successes, sent me as a day pupil to Robineau's—or, as we called it, Robinetto or Robinettino's—and made me take special private lessons from Pere Piquedent at the rate of five francs per hour, out of which the usher got two francs and the principal three francs. I was then eighteen, and was in the philosophy class.

These private lessons were given in a little room looking out on the street. It so happened that Pere Piquedent, instead of talking Latin to me, as he did when teaching publicly in the institution, kept telling me his troubles in French. Without relations, without friends, the poor man conceived an attachment to me, and poured out his misery to me.

He had never for the last ten or fifteen years chatted confidentially with any one.

"I am like an oak in a desert," he said—"'sicut quercus in solitudine'."

The other ushers disgusted him. He knew nobody in the town, since he had no time to devote to making acquaintances.

"Not even the nights, my friend, and that is the hardest thing on me. The dream of my life is to have a room with my own furniture, my own books, little things that belong to myself and which others may not touch. And I have nothing of my own, nothing except my trousers and my frock-coat, nothing, not even my mattress and my pillow! I have not four walls to shut myself up in, except when I come to give a lesson in this room. Do you see what this means—a man forced to spend his life without ever having the right, without ever finding the time, to shut himself up all alone, no matter where, to think, to reflect, to work, to dream? Ah! my dear boy, a key, the key of a door which one can lock—this is happiness, mark you, the only happiness!

"Here, all day long, teaching all those restless rogues, and during the night the dormitory with the same restless rogues snoring. And I have to sleep in the bed at the end of two rows of beds occupied by these youngsters whom I must look after. I can never be alone, never! If I go out I find the streets full of people, and, when I am tired of walking, I go into some cafe crowded with smokers and billiard players. I tell you what, it is the life of a galley slave."

I said:

"Why did you not take up some other line, Monsieur Piquedent?"

He exclaimed:

"What, my little friend? I am not a shoemaker, or a joiner, or a hatter, or a baker, or a hairdresser. I only know Latin, and I have no diploma which would enable me to sell my knowledge at a high price. If I were a doctor I would sell for a hundred francs what I now sell for a hundred sous; and I would supply it probably of an inferior quality, for my title would be enough to sustain my reputation."

Sometimes he would say to me:

"I have no rest in life except in the hours spent with you. Don't be afraid! you'll lose nothing by that. I'll make it up to you in the class-room by making you speak twice as much Latin as the others."

One day, I grew bolder, and offered him a cigarette. He stared at me in astonishment at first, then he gave a glance toward the door.

"If any one were to come in, my dear boy?"

"Well, let us smoke at the window," said I.

And we went and leaned our elbows on the windowsill looking on the street, holding concealed in our hands the little rolls of tobacco. Just opposite to us was a laundry. Four women in loose white waists were passing hot, heavy irons over the linen spread out before them, from which a warm steam arose.

Suddenly, another, a fifth, carrying on her arm a large basket which made her stoop, came out to take the customers their shirts, their handkerchiefs, and their sheets. She stopped on the threshold as if she were already fatigued; then, she raised her eyes, smiled as she saw us smoking, flung at us, with her left hand, which was free, the sly kiss characteristic of a free-and-easy working-woman, and went away at a slow place, dragging her feet as she went.

She was a woman of about twenty, small, rather thin, pale, rather pretty, with a roguish air and laughing eyes beneath her ill-combed fair hair.

Pere Piquedent, affected, began murmuring:

"What an occupation for a woman! Really a trade only fit for a horse."

And he spoke with emotion about the misery of the people. He had a heart which swelled with lofty democratic sentiment, and he referred to the fatiguing pursuits of the working class with phrases borrowed from Jean-Jacques Rousseau, and with sobs in his throat.

Next day, as we were leaning our elbows on the same window sill, the same woman perceived us and cried out to us:

"Good-day, scholars!" in a comical sort of tone, while she made a contemptuous gesture with her hands.

I flung her a cigarette, which she immediately began to smoke. And the four other ironers rushed out to the door with outstretched hands to get cigarettes also.

And each day a friendly intercourse was established between the working-women of the pavement and the idlers of the boarding school.

Pere Piquedent was really a comical sight. He trembled at being noticed, for he might lose his position; and he made timid and ridiculous gestures, quite a theatrical display of love signals, to which the women responded with a regular fusillade of kisses.

A perfidious idea came into my mind. One day, on entering our room, I said to the old usher in a low tone:

"You would not believe it, Monsieur Piquedent, I met the little washerwoman! You know the one I mean, the woman who had the basket, and I spoke to her!"

He asked, rather worried at my manner:

"What did she say to you?"

"She said to me—why, she said she thought you were very nice. The fact of the matter is, I believe, I believe, that she is a little in love with you." I saw that he was growing pale.

"She is laughing at me, of course. These things don't happen at my age," he replied.

I said gravely:

"How is that? You are all right."

As I felt that my trick had produced its effect on him, I did not press the matter.

But every day I pretended that I had met the little laundress and that I had spoken to her about him, so that in the end he believed me, and sent her ardent and earnest kisses.

Now it happened that one morning, on my way to the boarding school, I really came across her. I accosted her without hesitation, as if I had known her for the last ten years.

"Good-day, mademoiselle. Are you quite well?"

"Very well, monsieur, thank you."

"Will you have a cigarette?"

"Oh! not in the street."

"You can smoke it at home."

"In that case, I will."

"Let me tell you, mademoiselle, there's something you don't know."

"What is that, monsieur?"

"The old gentleman—my old professor, I mean—"

"Pere Piquedent?"

"Yes, Pere Piquedent. So you know his name?"

"Faith, I do! What of that?"

"Well, he is in love with you!"

She burst out laughing wildly, and exclaimed:

"You are only fooling."

"Oh! no, I am not fooling! He keeps talking of you all through the lesson. I bet that he'll marry you!"

She ceased laughing. The idea of marriage makes every girl serious. Then she repeated, with an incredulous air:

"This is humbug!"

"I swear to you, it's true."

She picked up her basket which she had laid down at her feet.

"Well, we'll see," she said. And she went away.

Presently when I had reached the boarding school, I took Pere Piquedent aside, and said:

"You must write to her; she is infatuated with you."

And he wrote a long letter, tenderly affectionate, full of phrases and circumlocutions, metaphors and similes, philosophy and academic gallantry; and I took on myself the responsibility of delivering it to the young woman.

She read it with gravity, with emotion; then she murmured:

"How well he writes! It is easy to see he has got education! Does he really mean to marry me?"

I replied intrepidly: "Faith, he has lost his head about you!"

"Then he must invite me to dinner on Sunday at the Ile des Fleurs."

I promised that she should be invited.

Pere Piquedent was much touched by everything I told him about her.

I added:

"She loves you, Monsieur Piquedent, and I believe her to be a decent girl. It is not right to lead her on and then abandon her."

He replied in a firm tone:

"I hope I, too, am a decent man, my friend."

I confess I had at the time no plan. I was playing a practical joke a schoolboy joke, nothing more. I had been aware of the simplicity of the old usher, his innocence and his weakness. I amused myself without asking myself how it would turn out. I was eighteen, and I had been for a long time looked upon at the lycee as a sly practical joker.

So it was agreed that Pere Piquedent and I should set out in a hack for the ferry of Queue de Vache, that we should there pick up Angele, and that I should take them into my boat, for in those days I was fond of boating. I would then bring them to the Ile des Fleurs, where the three of us would dine. I had inflicted myself on them, the better to enjoy my triumph, and the usher, consenting to my arrangement, proved clearly that he was losing his head by thus risking the loss of his position.

When we arrived at the ferry, where my boat had been moored since morning, I saw in the grass, or rather above the tall weeds of the bank, an enormous red parasol, resembling a monstrous wild poppy. Beneath the parasol was the little laundress in her Sunday clothes. I was surprised. She was really pretty, though pale; and graceful, though with a rather suburban grace.

Pere Piquedent raised his hat and bowed. She put out her hand toward him, and they stared at one another without uttering a word. Then they stepped into my boat, and I took the oars. They were seated side by side near the stern.

The usher was the first to speak.

"This is nice weather for a row in a boat."

She murmured:

"Oh! yes."

She dipped her hand into the water, skimming the surface, making a thin, transparent film like a sheet of glass, which made a soft plashing along the side of the boat.

When they were in the restaurant, she took it on herself to speak, and ordered dinner, fried fish, a chicken, and salad; then she led us on toward the isle, which she knew perfectly.

After this, she was gay, romping, and even rather tantalizing.

Until dessert, no question of love arose. I had treated them to champagne, and Pere Piquedent was tipsy. Herself slightly the worse, she called out to him:

"Monsieur Piquenez."

He said abruptly:

"Mademoiselle, Monsieur Raoul has communicated my sentiments to you."

She became as serious as a judge.

"Yes, monsieur."

"What is your reply?"

"We never reply to these questions!"

He puffed with emotion, and went on:

"Well, will the day ever come that you will like me?"

She smiled.

"You big stupid! You are very nice."

"In short, mademoiselle, do you think that, later on, we might—"

She hesitated a second; then in a trembling voice she said:

"Do you mean to marry me when you say that? For on no other condition, you know."

"Yes, mademoiselle!"

"Well, that's all right, Monsieur Piquedent!"

It was thus that these two silly creatures promised marriage to each other through the trick of a young scamp. But I did not believe that it was serious, nor, indeed, did they, perhaps.

"You know, I have nothing, not four sous," she said.

He stammered, for he was as drunk as Silenus:

"I have saved five thousand francs."

She exclaimed triumphantly:

"Then we can set up in business?"

He became restless.

"In what business?"

"What do I know? We shall see. With five thousand francs we could do many things. You don't want me to go and live in your boarding school, do you?"

He had not looked forward so far as this, and he stammered in great perplexity:

"What business could we set up in? That would not do, for all I know is Latin!"

She reflected in her turn, passing in review all her business ambitions.

"You could not be a doctor?"

"No, I have no diploma."

"Or a chemist?"

"No more than the other."

She uttered a cry of joy. She had discovered it.

"Then we'll buy a grocer's shop! Oh! what luck! we'll buy a grocer's shop. Not on a big scale, of course; with five thousand francs one does not go far."

He was shocked at the suggestion.

"No, I can't be a grocer. I am—I am—too well known: I only know Latin, that is all I know."

But she poured a glass of champagne down his throat. He drank it and was silent.

We got back into the boat. The night was dark, very dark. I saw clearly, however, that he had caught her by the waist, and that they were hugging each other again and again.

It was a frightful catastrophe. Our escapade was discovered, with the result that Pere Piquedent was dismissed. And my father, in a fit of anger, sent me to finish my course of philosophy at Ribaudet's school.

Six months later I took my degree of Bachelor of Arts. Then I went to study law in Paris, and did not return to my native town till two years later.

At the corner of the Rue de Serpent a shop caught my eye. Over the door were the words: "Colonial Products—Piquedent"; then underneath, so as to enlighten the most ignorant: "Grocery."

I exclaimed:

"'Quantum mutatus ab illo!'"

Piquedent raised his head, left his female customer, and rushed toward me with outstretched hands.

"Ah! my young friend, my young friend, here you are! What luck! what luck!"

A beautiful woman, very plump, abruptly left the cashier's desk and flung herself on my breast. I had some difficulty in recognizing her, she had grown so stout.

I asked:

"So then you're doing well?"

Piquedent had gone back to weigh the groceries.

"Oh! very well, very well, very well. I have made three thousand francs clear this year!"

"And what about Latin, Monsieur Piquedent?"

"Oh, good heavens! Latin, Latin, Latin—you see it does not keep the pot boiling!"

A MEETING

*J*t was nothing but an accident, an accident pure and simple. On that particular evening the princess' rooms were open, and as they appeared dark after the brilliantly lighted parlors, Baron d'Etraille, who was tired of standing, inadvertently wandered into an empty bedroom.

He looked round for a chair in which to have a doze, as he was sure his wife would not leave before daylight. As soon as he became accustomed to the light of the room he distinguished the big bed with its azure-and-gold hangings, in the middle of the great room, looking like a catafalque in which love was buried, for the princess was no longer young. Behind it, a large bright surface looked like a lake seen at a distance. It was a large mirror, discreetly covered with dark drapery, that was very rarely let down, and seemed to look at the bed, which was its accomplice. One might almost fancy that it had reminiscences, and that one might see in it charming female forms and the gentle movement of loving arms.

The baron stood still for a moment, smiling, almost experiencing an emotion on the threshold of this chamber dedicated to love. But suddenly something appeared in the looking-glass, as if the phantoms which he had evoked had risen up before him. A man and a woman who had been sitting on a low couch concealed in the shadow had arisen, and the polished surface, reflecting their figures, showed that they were kissing each other before separating.

Baron d'Etraille recognized his wife and the Marquis de Cervigne. He turned and went away like a man who is fully master of himself, and waited till it was day before taking away the baroness; but he had no longer any thoughts of sleeping.

As soon as they were alone he said:

"Madame, I saw you just now in Princesse de Raynes' room; I need say no more, and I am not fond either of reproaches, acts of violence, or of ridicule. As I wish to avoid all such things, we shall separate without any scandal. Our lawyers will settle your position according to my orders. You will be free to live as you please when you are no longer under my roof; but, as you will continue to bear my name, I must warn you that should any scandal arise I shall show myself inflexible."

She tried to speak, but he stopped her, bowed, and left the room.

He was more astonished and sad than unhappy. He had loved her dearly during the first period of their married life; but his ardor had cooled, and now he often amused himself elsewhere, either in a theatre or in society, though he always preserved a certain liking for the baroness.

She was very young, hardly four-and-twenty, small, slight—too slight—and very fair. She was a true Parisian doll: clever, spoiled, elegant, coquettish, witty, with more charm than real beauty. He used to say familiarly to his brother, when speaking of her:

"My wife is charming, attractive, but—there is nothing to lay hold of. She is like a glass of champagne that is all froth; when you get to the wine it is very good, but there is too little of it, unfortunately."

He walked up and down the room in great agitation, thinking of a thousand things. At one moment he was furious, and felt inclined to give the marquis a good thrashing, or to slap his face publicly, in the club. But he decided that would not do, it would not be good form; he would be laughed at, and not his rival, and this thought wounded his vanity. So he went to bed, but could not sleep. Paris knew in a few days that the Baron and Baroness d'Etraille had agreed to an amicable separation on account of incompatibility of temper. No one suspected anything, no one laughed, and no one was astonished.

The baron, however, to avoid meeting his wife, travelled for a year, then spent the summer at the seaside, and the autumn in shooting, returning to Paris for the winter. He did not meet the baroness once.

He did not even know what people said about her. In any case, she took care to respect appearances, and that was all he asked for.

He became dreadfully bored, travelled again, restored his old castle of Villebosc, which took him two years; then for over a year he entertained friends there, till at last, tired of all these so-called pleasures, he returned to his mansion in the Rue de Lille, just six years after the separation.

He was now forty-five, with a good crop of gray hair, rather stout, and with that melancholy look characteristic of those who have been handsome, sought after, and liked, but who are deteriorating, daily.

A month after his return to Paris, he took cold on coming out of his club, and had such a bad cough that his medical man ordered him to Nice for the rest of the winter.

He reached the station only a few minutes before the departure of the train on Monday evening, and had barely time to get into a carriage, with only one other occupant, who was sitting in a corner so wrapped in furs and cloaks that he could not even make out whether it was a man or a woman, as nothing of the figure could be seen. When he perceived that he could not find out, he put on his travelling cap, rolled himself up in his rugs, and stretched out comfortably to sleep.

He did not wake until the day was breaking, and looked at once at his fellow-traveller, who had not stirred all night, and seemed still to be sound asleep.

M. d'Etraille made use of the opportunity to brush his hair and his beard, and to try to freshen himself up a little generally, for a night's travel does not improve one's appearance when one has attained a certain age.

A great poet has said:

"When we are young, our mornings are triumphant!"

Then we wake up with a cool skin, a bright eye, and glossy hair.

As one grows older one wakes up in a very different condition. Dull eyes, red, swollen cheeks, dry lips, hair and beard disarranged, impart an old, fatigued, worn-out look to the face.

The baron opened his travelling case, and improved his looks as much as possible.

The engine whistled, the train stopped, and his neighbor moved. No doubt he was awake. They started off again, and then a slanting ray of sunlight shone into the carriage and on the sleeper, who moved again, shook himself, and then his face could be seen.

It was a young, fair, pretty, plump woman, and the baron looked at her in amazement. He did not know what to think. He could really have sworn that it was his wife, but wonderfully changed for the better: stouter —why she had grown as stout as he was, only it suited her much better than it did him.

She looked at him calmly, did not seem to recognize him, and then slowly laid aside her wraps. She had that quiet assurance of a woman who is sure of herself, who feels that on awaking she is in her full beauty and freshness.

The baron was really bewildered. Was it his wife, or else as like her as any sister could be? Not having seen her for six years, he might be mistaken.

She yawned, and this gesture betrayed her. She turned and

looked at him again, calmly, indifferently, as if she scarcely saw him, and then looked out of the window again.

He was upset and dreadfully perplexed, and kept looking at her sideways.

Yes; it was surely his wife. How could he possibly have doubted it? There could certainly not be two noses like that, and a thousand recollections flashed through his mind. He felt the old feeling of the intoxication of love stealing over him, and he called to mind the sweet odor of her skin, her smile when she put her arms on to his shoulders, the soft intonations of her voice, all her graceful, coaxing ways.

But how she had changed and improved! It was she and yet not she. She seemed riper, more developed, more of a woman, more seductive, more desirable, adorably desirable.

And this strange, unknown woman, whom he had accidentally met in a railway carriage, belonged to him; he had only to say to her:

"I insist upon it."

He had formerly slept in her arms, existed only in her love, and now he had found her again certainly, but so changed that he scarcely knew her. It was another, and yet it was she herself. It was some one who had been born and had formed and grown since he had left her. It was she, indeed; she whom he had loved, but who was now altered, with a more assured smile and greater self-possession. There were two women in one, mingling a great part of what was new and unknown with many sweet recollections of the past. There was something singular, disturbing, exciting about it —a kind of mystery of love in which there floated a delicious confusion. It was his wife in a new body and in new flesh which lips had never pressed.

And he thought that in a few years nearly every thing changes in us; only the outline can be recognized, and sometimes even that disappears.

The blood, the hair, the skin, all changes and is renewed, and when people have not seen each other for a long time, when they meet they find each other totally different beings, although they are the same and bear the same name.

And the heart also can change. Ideas may be modified and renewed, so that in forty years of life we may, by gradual and constant transformations, become four or five totally new and different beings.

He dwelt on this thought till it troubled him; it had first taken possession of him when he surprised her in the princess' room.

He was not the least angry; it was not the same woman that he was looking at —that thin, excitable little doll of those days.

What was he to do? How should he address her? and what could he say to her? Had she recognized him?

The train stopped again. He got up, bowed, and said: "Bertha, do you want anything I could bring you?"

She looked at him from head to foot, and answered, without showing the slightest surprise, or confusion, or anger, but with the most perfect indifference:

"I do not want anything—-thank you."

He got out and walked up and down the platform a little in order to recover himself, and, as it were, to recover his senses after a fall. What should he do now? If he got into another carriage it would look as if he were running away. Should he be polite or importunate? That would look as if he were asking for forgiveness. Should he speak as if he were her master? He would look like a fool, and, besides, he really had no right to do so.

He got in again and took his place.

During his absence she had hastily arranged her dress and hair, and was now lying stretched out on the seat, radiant, and without showing any emotion.

He turned to her, and said: "My dear Bertha, since this singular chance has brought up together after a separation of six years—a quite friendly separation—are we to continue to look upon each other as irreconcilable enemies? We are shut up together, tete-a-tete, which is so much the better or so much the worse. I am not going to get into another carriage, so don't you think it is preferable to talk as friends till the end of our journey?"

She answered, quite calmly again:

"Just as you please."

Then he suddenly stopped, really not knowing what to say; but as he had plenty of assurance, he sat down on the middle seat, and said:

"Well, I see I must pay my court to you; so much the better. It is, however, really a pleasure, for you are charming. You cannot imagine how you have improved in the last six years. I do not know any woman who could give me that delightful sensation which I experienced just now when you emerged from your wraps. I really could not have thought such a change possible."

Without moving her head or looking at him, she said: "I cannot say the same with regard to you; you have certainly deteriorated a great deal."

He got red and confused, and then, with a smile of resignation, he said:

"You are rather hard."

"Why?" was her reply. "I am only stating facts. I don't suppose you intend to offer me your love? It must, therefore, be a matter of perfect indifference to you what I think about you. But I see it is a painful subject, so let us talk of something else. What have you been doing since I last saw you?"

He felt rather out of countenance, and stammered:

"I? I have travelled, done some shooting, and grown old, as you see. And you?"

She said, quite calmly: "I have taken care of appearances, as you ordered me."

He was very nearly saying something brutal, but he checked himself; and kissed his wife's hand:

"And I thank you," he said.

She was surprised. He was indeed diplomatic, and always master of himself.

He went on: "As you have acceded to my first request, shall we now talk without any bitterness?"

She made a little movement of surprise.

"Bitterness? I don't feel any; you are a complete stranger to me; I am only trying to keep up a difficult conversation."

He was still looking at her, fascinated in spite of her harshness, and he felt seized with a brutal Beside, the desire of the master.

Perceiving that she had hurt his feelings, she said:

"How old are you now? I thought you were younger than you look."

"I am forty-five"; and then he added: "I forgot to ask after Princesse de Raynes. Are you still intimate with her?"

She looked at him as if she hated him:

"Yes, I certainly am. She is very well, thank you."

They remained sitting side by side, agitated and irritated. Suddenly he said:

"My dear Bertha, I have changed my mind. You are my wife, and I expect you to come with me to-day. You have, I think, improved both morally and physically, and I am going to take you back again. I am your husband, and it is my right to do so."

She was stupefied, and looked at him, trying to divine his thoughts; but his face was resolute and impenetrable.

"I am very sorry," she said, "but I have made other engagements."

"So much the worse for you," was his reply. "The law gives me the power, and I mean to use it."

They were nearing Marseilles, and the train whistled and slackened speed. The baroness rose, carefully rolled up her wraps, and then, turning to her husband, said:

"My dear Raymond, do not make a bad use of this tete-a tete which I had carefully prepared. I wished to take precautions, according to your advice, so that I might have nothing to fear from you or from other people, whatever might happen. You are going to Nice, are you not?"

"I shall go wherever you go."

"Not at all; just listen to me, and I am sure that you will leave me in peace. In a few moments, when we get to the station, you will see the Princesse de Raynes and Comtesse Henriot waiting for me with their husbands. I wished them to see as, and to know that we had spent the night together in the railway carriage. Don't be alarmed; they will tell it everywhere as a most surprising fact.

"I told you just now that I had most carefully followed your advice and saved appearances. Anything else does not matter, does it? Well, in order to do so, I wished to be seen with you. You told me carefully to avoid any scandal, and I am avoiding it, for, I am afraid—I am afraid—"

She waited till the train had quite stopped, and as her friends ran up to open the carriage door, she said:

"I am afraid"—hesitating—"that there is another reason—je suis enceinte."

The princess stretched out her arms to embrace her,—and the baroness said, painting to the baron, who was dumb with astonishment, and was trying to get at the truth:

"You do not recognize Raymond? He has certainly changed a good deal, and he agreed to come with me so that I might not travel alone. We take little trips like this occasionally, like good friends who cannot live together. We are going to separate here; he has had enough of me already."

She put out her hand, which he took mechanically, and then she jumped out on to the platform among her friends, who were waiting for her.

The baron hastily shut the carriage door, for he was too much disturbed to say a word or come to any determination. He heard his wife's voice and their merry laughter as they went away.

He never saw her again, nor did he ever discover whether she had told him a lie or was speaking the truth.

THE BLIND MAN

How is it that the sunlight gives us such joy? Why does this radiance when it falls on the earth fill us with the joy of living? The whole sky is blue, the fields are green, the houses all white, and our enchanted eyes drink in those bright colors which bring delight to our souls. And then there springs up in our hearts a desire to dance, to run, to sing, a happy lightness of thought, a sort of enlarged tenderness; we feel a longing to embrace the sun.

The blind, as they sit in the doorways, impassive in their eternal darkness, remain as calm as ever in the midst of this fresh gaiety, and, not understanding what is taking place around them, they continually check their dogs as they attempt to play.

When, at the close of the day, they are returning home on the arm of a young brother or a little sister, if the child says: "It was a very fine day!" the other answers: "I could notice that it was fine. Loulou wouldn't keep quiet."

I knew one of these men whose life was one of the most cruel martyrdoms that could possibly be conceived.

He was a peasant, the son of a Norman farmer. As long as his father and mother lived, he was more or less taken care of; he suffered little save from his horrible infirmity; but as soon as the old people were gone, an atrocious life of misery commenced for him. Dependent on a sister of his, everybody in the farmhouse treated him as a beggar who is eating the bread of strangers. At every meal the very food he swallowed was made a subject of reproach against him; he was called a drone, a clown, and although his brother-in-law had taken possession of his portion of the inheritance, he was helped grudgingly to soup, getting just enough to save him from starving.

His face was very pale and his two big white eyes looked like wafers. He remained unmoved at all the insults hurled at him, so reserved that one could not tell whether he felt them.

Moreover, he had never known any tenderness, his mother having always treated him unkindly and caring very little for him; for in country places useless persons are considered a nuisance, and the peasants would be glad to kill the infirm of their species, as poultry do.

As soon as he finished his soup he went and sat outside the door in summer and in winter beside the fireside, and did not stir again all the evening. He made no gesture, no movement; only his eyelids, quivering from some nervous affection, fell down sometimes over his white, sightless orbs. Had he any intellect, any thinking faculty, any consciousness of his own existence? Nobody cared to inquire.

For some years things went on in this fashion. But his incapacity for work as well as his impassiveness eventually exasperated his relatives, and he became a laughingstock, a sort of butt for merriment, a prey to the inborn ferocity, to the savage gaiety of the brutes who surrounded him.

It is easy to imagine all the cruel practical jokes inspired by his blindness. And, in order to have some fun in return for feeding him, they now converted his meals into hours of pleasure for the neighbors and of punishment for the helpless creature himself.

The peasants from the nearest houses came to this entertainment; it was talked about from door to door, and every day the kitchen of the farmhouse was full of people. Sometimes they placed before his plate, when he was beginning to eat his soup, some cat or dog. The animal instinctively perceived the man's infirmity, and, softly approaching, commenced eating noiselessly, lapping up the soup daintily; and, when they lapped the food rather noisily, rousing the poor fellow's attention, they would prudently scamper away to avoid the blow of the spoon directed at random by the blind man!

Then the spectators ranged along the wall would burst out laughing, nudge each other and stamp their feet on the floor. And he, without ever uttering a word, would continue eating with his right hand, while stretching out his left to protect his plate.

Another time they made him chew corks, bits of wood, leaves or even filth, which he was unable to distinguish.

After this they got tired even of these practical jokes, and the brother-in-law, angry at having to support him always, struck him, cuffed him incessantly, laughing at his futile efforts to ward off or return the blows. Then came a new pleasure—the pleasure of smacking his face. And the plough-men, the servant girls and even every passing vagabond were every moment giving him cuffs, which caused his eyelashes to twitch spasmodically. He did not know where to hide himself and remained with his arms always held out to guard against people coming too close to him.

At last he was forced to beg.

He was placed somewhere on the high-road on market-days, and as soon as he heard the sound of footsteps or the rolling of a vehicle, he reached out his hat, stammering:

"Charity, if you please!"

But the peasant is not lavish, and for whole weeks he did not bring back a sou.

Then he became the victim of furious, pitiless hatred. And this is how he died.

One winter the ground was covered with snow, and it was freezing hard. His brother-in-law led him one morning a great distance along the high road in order that he might solicit alms. The blind man was left there all day; and when night came on, the brother-in-law told the people of his house that he could find no trace of the mendicant. Then he added:

"Pooh! best not bother about him! He was cold and got someone to take him away. Never fear! he's not lost. He'll turn up soon enough tomorrow to eat the soup."

Next day he did not come back.

After long hours of waiting, stiffened with the cold, feeling that he was dying, the blind man began to walk. Being unable to find his way along the road, owing to its thick coating of ice, he went on at random, falling into ditches, getting up again, without uttering a sound, his sole object being to find some house where he could take shelter.

But, by degrees, the descending snow made a numbness steal over him, and his feeble limbs being incapable of carrying him farther, he sat down in the middle of an open field. He did not get up again.

The white flakes which fell continuously buried him, so that his body, quite stiff and stark, disappeared under the incessant accumulation of their rapidly thickening mass, and nothing was left to indicate the place where he lay.

His relatives made a pretence of inquiring about him and searching for him for about a week. They even made a show of weeping.

The winter was severe, and the thaw did not set in quickly. Now, one Sunday, on their way to mass, the farmers noticed a great flight of crows, who were whirling incessantly above the open field, and then descending like a shower of black rain at the same spot, ever going and coming.

The following week these gloomy birds were still there. There was a crowd of them up in the air, as if they had gathered from all corners of the horizon, and they swooped down with a great cawing into the shining snow, which they covered like black patches, and in which they kept pecking obstinately. A young fellow went to see what they were doing and discovered the body of the blind man, already half devoured, mangled. His wan eyes had disappeared, pecked out by the long, voracious beaks.

And I can never feel the glad radiance of sunlit days without sadly remembering and pondering over the fate of the beggar who was such an outcast in life that his horrible death was a relief to all who had known him.

INDISCRETION

They had loved each other before marriage with a pure and lofty love. They had first met on the seashore. He had thought this young girl charming, as she passed by with her light-colored parasol and her dainty dress amid the marine landscape against the horizon. He had loved her, blond and slender, in these surroundings of blue ocean and spacious sky. He could not distinguish the tenderness which this budding woman awoke in him from the vague and powerful emotion which the fresh salt air and the grand scenery of surf and sunshine and waves aroused in his soul.

She, on the other hand, had loved him because he courted her, because he was young, rich, kind, and attentive. She had loved him because it is natural for young girls to love men who whisper sweet nothings to them.

So, for three months, they had lived side by side, and hand in hand. The greeting which they exchanged in the morning before the bath, in the freshness of the morning, or in the evening on the sand, under the stars, in the warmth of a calm night, whispered low, very low, already had the flavor of kisses, though their lips had never met.

Each dreamed of the other at night, each thought of the other on awaking, * and, without yet having voiced their sentiments, each longing for the other, body and soul.

After marriage their love descended to earth. It was at first a tireless, sensuous passion, then exalted tenderness composed of tangible poetry, more refined caresses, and new and foolish inventions. Every glance and gesture was an expression of passion.

But, little by little, without even noticing it, they began to get tired of each other. Love was still strong, but they had nothing more to reveal to each other, nothing more to learn from each other, no new tale of endearment, no unexpected outburst, no new way of expressing the well-known, oft-repeated verb.

They tried, however, to rekindle the dwindling flame of the first love. Every day they tried some new trick or desperate attempt to bring back to their hearts the uncooled ardor of their first days of married life. They tried moonlight walks under the trees, in the sweet warmth of the summer evenings: the poetry of mist-covered beaches; the excitement of public festivals.

One morning Henriette said to Paul:

"Will you take me to a cafe for dinner?"

"Certainly, dearie."

"To some well-known cafe?"

"Of course!"

He looked at her with a questioning glance, seeing that she was thinking of something which she did not wish to tell.

She went on:

"You know, one of those cafes—oh, how can I explain myself?—a sporty cafe!"

He smiled: "Of course, I understand—you mean in one of the cafes which are commonly called bohemian."

"Yes, that's it. But take me to one of the big places, one where you are known, one where you have already supped—no—dined—well, you know—I—I—oh! I will never dare say it!"

"Go ahead, dearie. Little secrets should no longer exist between us."

"No, I dare not."

"Go on; don't be prudish. Tell me."

"Well, I—I—I want to be taken for your sweetheart—there! and I want the boys, who do not know that you are married, to take me for such; and you too—I want you to think that I am your sweetheart for one hour, in that place which must hold so many memories for you. There! And I will play that I am your sweetheart. It's awful, I know—I am abominably ashamed, I am as red as a peony. Don't look at me!"

He laughed, greatly amused, and answered:

"All right, we will go to-night to a very swell place where I am well known."

Toward seven o'clock they went up the stairs of one of the big cafes on the Boulevard, he, smiling, with the look of a conqueror, she, timid, veiled, delighted. They were immediately shown to one of the luxurious private dining-rooms, furnished with four large arm-chairs and a red plush couch. The head waiter entered and brought them the menu. Paul handed it to his wife.

"What do you want to eat?"

"I don't care; order whatever is good."

After handing his coat to the waiter, he ordered dinner and champagne. The waiter looked at the young woman and smiled.

He took the order and murmured:

"Will Monsieur Paul have his champagne sweet or dry?"

"Dry, very dry."

Henriette was pleased to hear that this man knew her husband's name. They sat on the couch, side by side, and began to eat.

Ten candles lighted the room and were reflected in the mirrors all around them, which seemed to increase the brilliancy a thousand-fold. Henriette drank glass after glass in order to keep up her courage, although she felt dizzy after the first few glasses. Paul, excited by the memories which returned to him, kept kissing his wife's hands. His eyes were sparkling.

She was feeling strangely excited in this new place, restless, pleased, a little guilty, but full of life. Two waiters, serious, silent, accustomed to seeing and forgetting everything, to entering the room only when it was necessary and to leaving it when they felt they were intruding, were silently flitting hither and thither.

Toward the middle of the dinner, Henriette was well under the influence of champagne. She was prattling along fearlessly, her cheeks flushed, her eyes glistening.

"Come, Paul; tell me everything."

"What, sweetheart?"

"I don't dare tell you."

"Go on!"

"Have you loved many women before me?"

He hesitated, a little perplexed, not knowing whether he should hide his adventures or boast of them.

She continued:

"Oh! please tell me. How many have you loved?"

"A few."

"How many?"

"I don't know. How do you expect me to know such things?"

"Haven't you counted them?"

"Of course not."

"Then you must have loved a good many!"

"Perhaps."

"About how many? Just tell me about how many."

"But I don't know, dearest. Some years a good many, and some years only a few."

"How many a year, did you say?"

"Sometimes twenty or thirty, sometimes only four or five."

"Oh! that makes more than a hundred in all!"

"Yes, just about."

"Oh! I think that is dreadful!"

"Why dreadful?"

"Because it's dreadful when you think of it—all those women—and always—always the same thing. Oh! it's dreadful, just the same—more than a hundred women!"

He was surprised that she should think that dreadful, and answered, with the air of superiority which men take with women when they wish to make them understand that they have said something foolish:

"That's funny! If it is dreadful to have a hundred women, it's dreadful to have one."

"Oh, no, not at all!"

"Why not?"

"Because with one woman you have a real bond of love which attaches you to her, while with a hundred women it's not the same at all. There is no real love. I don't understand how a man can associate with such women."

"But they are all right."

"No, they can't be!"

"Yes, they are!"

"Oh, stop; you disgust me!"

"But then, why did you ask me how many sweethearts I had had?"

"Because——"

"That's no reason!"

"What were they-actresses, little shop-girls, or society women?"

"A few of each."

"It must have been rather monotonous toward the last."

"Oh, no; it's amusing to change."

She remained thoughtful, staring at her champagne glass. It was full —she drank it in one gulp; then putting it back on the table, she threw her arms around her husband's neck and murmured in his ear:

"Oh! how I love you, sweetheart! how I love you!"

He threw his arms around her in a passionate embrace. A waiter, who was just entering, backed out, closing the door discreetly. In about five minutes the head waiter came back, solemn and dignified, bringing the fruit for dessert. She was once more holding between her fingers a full glass, and gazing into the amber liquid as though seeking unknown things. She murmured in a dreamy voice:

"Yes, it must be fun!"

A FAMILY AFFAIR

The small engine attached to the Neuilly steam-tram whistled as it passed the Porte Maillot to warn all obstacles to get out of its way and puffed like a person out of breath as it sent out its steam, its pistons moving rapidly with a noise as of iron legs running. The train was going along the broad avenue that ends at the Seine. The sultry heat at the close of a July day lay over the whole city, and from the road, although there was not a breath of wind stirring, there arose a white, chalky, suffocating, warm dust, which adhered to the moist skin, filled the eyes and got into the lungs. People stood in the doorways of their houses to try and get a breath of air.

The windows of the steam-tram were open and the curtains fluttered in the wind. There were very few passengers inside, because on warm days people preferred the outside or the platforms. They consisted of stout women in peculiar costumes, of those shopkeepers' wives from the suburbs, who made up for the distinguished looks which they did not possess by ill-assumed dignity; of men tired from office-work, with yellow faces, stooped shoulders, and with one shoulder higher than the other, in consequence of, their long hours of writing at a desk. Their uneasy and melancholy faces also spoke of domestic troubles, of constant want of money, disappointed hopes, for they all belonged to the army of poor, threadbare devils who vegetate economically in cheap, plastered houses with a tiny piece of neglected garden on the outskirts of Paris, in the midst of those fields where night soil is deposited.

A short, corpulent man, with a puffy face, dressed all in black and wearing a decoration in his buttonhole, was talking to a tall, thin man, dressed in a dirty, white linen suit, the coat all unbuttoned, with a white Panama hat on his head. The former spoke so slowly and hesitatingly that it occasionally almost seemed as if he stammered; he was Monsieur Caravan, chief clerk in the Admiralty. The other, who had formerly been surgeon on board a merchant ship, had set up in practice in Courbevoie, where he applied the vague remnants of medical knowledge which he had retained after an adventurous life, to the wretched population of that district. His name was Chenet, and strange rumors were current as to his morality.

Monsieur Caravan had always led the normal life of a man in a Government office. For the last thirty years he had invariably gone the same way to his office every morning, and had met the same men going to business at the same time, and nearly on the same spot, and he returned home every evening by the same road, and again met the same faces which he had seen growing old. Every morning, after buying his penny paper at the corner of the Faubourg Saint Honore, he bought two rolls, and then went to his office, like a culprit who is giving himself up to justice, and got to his desk as quickly as possible, always feeling uneasy; as though he were expecting a rebuke for some neglect of duty of which he might have been guilty.

Nothing had ever occurred to change the monotonous order of his existence, for no event affected him except the work of his office, perquisites, gratuities, and promotion. He never spoke of anything but of his duties, either at the office, or at home—he had married the portionless daughter of one of his colleagues. His mind, which was in a state of atrophy from his depressing daily work, had no other thoughts, hopes or dreams than such as related to the office, and there was a constant source of bitterness that spoilt every pleasure that he might have had, and that was the employment of so many naval officials, tinsmiths, as they were called because of their silver-lace as first-class clerks; and every evening at dinner he discussed the matter hotly with his wife, who shared his angry feelings, and proved to their own satisfaction that it was in every way unjust to give places in Paris to men who ought properly to have been employed in the navy.

He was old now, and had scarcely noticed how his life was passing, for school had merely been exchanged for the office without any intermediate transition, and the ushers, at whom he had formerly trembled, were replaced by his chiefs, of whom he was terribly afraid. When he had to go into the rooms of these official despots, it made him tremble from head to foot, and that constant fear had given him a very awkward manner in their presence, a humble demeanor, and a kind of nervous stammering.

He knew nothing more about Paris than a blind man might know who was led to the same spot by his dog every day; and if he read the account of any uncommon events or scandals in his penny paper, they appeared to him like fantastic tales, which some pressman had made up out of his own head, in order to amuse the inferior employees. He did not read the political news, which his paper frequently altered as the cause which subsidized it might require, for he was not fond of innovations, and when he went through the Avenue of the Champs-Elysees every evening, he looked at the surging crowd of pedestrians, and at the stream of carriages, as a traveller might who has lost his way in a strange country.

As he had completed his thirty years of obligatory service that year, on the first of January, he had had the cross of the Legion of Honor bestowed upon him, which, in the semi-military public offices, is a recompense for the miserable slavery—the official phrase is, loyal services—of unfortunate convicts who are riveted to their desk. That unexpected dignity gave him a high and new idea of his own capacities, and altogether changed him. He immediately left off wearing light trousers and fancy waistcoats, and wore black trousers and long coats, on which his ribbon, which was very broad, showed off better. He got shaved every morning, manicured his nails more carefully, changed his linen every two days, from a legitimate sense of what was proper, and out of respect for the national Order, of which he formed a part, and from that day he was another Caravan, scrupulously clean, majestic and condescending.

At home, he said, "my cross," at every moment, and he had become so proud of it, that he could not bear to see men wearing any other ribbon in their button-holes. He became especially angry on seeing strange orders: "Which nobody ought to be allowed to wear in France," and he bore Chenet a particular grudge, as he met him on a tram-car every evening, wearing a decoration of one kind or another, white, blue, orange, or green.

The conversation of the two men, from the Arc de Triomphe to Neuilly, was always the same, and on that day they discussed, first of all, various local abuses which disgusted them both, and the Mayor of Neuilly received his full share of their censure. Then, as invariably happens in the company of medical men, Caravan began to enlarge on the chapter of illness, as in that manner, he hoped to obtain a little gratuitous advice, if he was careful not to show his hand. His mother had been causing him no little anxiety for some time; she had frequent and prolonged fainting fits, and, although she was ninety, she would not take care of herself.

Caravan grew quite tender-hearted when he mentioned her great age, and more than once asked Doctor Chenet, emphasizing the word doctor—although he was not fully qualified, being only an Offcier de Sante—whether he had often met anyone as old as that. And he rubbed his hands with pleasure; not, perhaps, that he cared very much about seeing the good woman last forever here on earth, but because the long duration of his mother's life was, as it were an earnest of old age for himself, and he continued:

"In my family, we last long, and I am sure that, unless I meet with an accident, I shall not die until I am very old."

The doctor looked at him with pity, and glanced for a moment at his neighbor's red face, his short, thick neck, his "corporation," as Chenet called it to himself, his two fat, flabby legs, and the apoplectic rotundity of the old official; and raising the white Panama hat from his head, he said with a snigger:

"I am not so sure of that, old fellow; your mother is as tough as nails, and I should say that your life is not a very good one."

This rather upset Caravan, who did not speak again until the tram put them down at their destination, where the two friends got out, and Chenet asked his friend to have a glass of vermouth at the Cafe du Globe, opposite, which both of them were in the habit of frequenting. The proprietor, who was a friend of theirs, held out to them two fingers, which they shook across the bottles of the counter; and then they joined three of their friends, who were playing dominoes, and who had been there since midday. They exchanged cordial greetings, with the usual question: "Anything new?" And then the three players continued their game, and held out their hands without looking up, when the others wished them "Good-night," and then they both went home to dinner.

Caravan lived in a small two-story house in Courbevaie, near where the roads meet; the ground floor was occupied by a hair-dresser. Two bed rooms, a dining-room and a kitchen, formed the whole of their apartments, and Madame Caravan spent nearly her whole time in cleaning them up, while her daughter, Marie-Louise, who was twelve, and her son, Phillip-Auguste, were running about with all the little, dirty, mischievous brats of the neighborhood, and playing in the gutter.

Caravan had installed his mother, whose avarice was notorious in the neighborhood, and who was terribly thin, in the room above them. She was always cross, and she never passed a day without quarreling and flying into furious tempers. She would apostrophize the neighbors, who were standing at their own doors, the coster-mongers, the street-sweepers, and the street-boys, in the most violent language; and the latter, to have their revenge, used to follow her at a distance when she went out, and call out rude things after her.

A little servant from Normandy, who was incredibly giddy and thoughtless, performed the household work, and slept on the second floor in the same room as the old woman, for fear of anything happening to her in the night.

When Caravan got in, his wife, who suffered from a chronic passion for cleaning, was polishing up the mahogany chairs that were scattered about the room with a piece of flannel. She always wore cotton gloves, and adorned her head with a cap ornamented with many colored ribbons, which was always tilted over one ear; and whenever anyone caught her polishing, sweeping, or washing, she used to say:

"I am not rich; everything is very simple in my house, but cleanliness is my luxury, and that is worth quite as much as any other."

As she was gifted with sound, obstinate, practical common sense, she led her husband in everything. Every evening during dinner, and afterwards when they were in their room, they talked over the business of the office for a long time, and although she was twenty years younger than he was, he confided everything to her as if she took the lead, and followed her advice in every matter.

She had never been pretty, and now she had grown ugly; in addition to that, she was short and thin, while her careless and tasteless way of dressing herself concealed her few small feminine attractions, which might have been brought out if she had possessed any taste in dress. Her skirts were always awry, and she frequently scratched herself, no matter on what part of her person, totally indifferent as to who might see her, and so persistently, that anyone who saw her might think that she was suffering from something like the itch. The only adornments that she allowed herself were silk ribbons, which she had in great profusion, and of various colors mixed together, in the pretentious caps which she wore at home.

As soon as she saw her husband she rose and said, as she kissed his whiskers:

"Did you remember Potin, my dear?"

He fell into a chair, in consternation, for that was the fourth time on which he had forgotten a commission that he had promised to do for her.

"It is a fatality," he said; "it is no good for me to think of it all day long, for I am sure to forget it in the evening."

But as he seemed really so very sorry, she merely said, quietly:

"You will think of it to-morrow, I dare say. Anything new at the office?"

"Yes, a great piece of news; another tinsmith has been appointed second chief clerk." She became very serious, and said:

"So he succeeds Ramon; this was the very post that I wanted you to have. And what about Ramon?"

"He retires on his pension."

She became furious, her cap slid down on her shoulder, and she continued:

"There is nothing more to be done in that shop now. And what is the name of the new commissioner?"

"Bonassot."

She took up the Naval Year Book, which she always kept close at hand, and looked him up.

"'Bonassot-Toulon. Born in 1851. Student Commissioner in 1871. Sub-Commissioner in 1875.' Has he been to sea?" she continued. At that question Caravan's looks cleared up, and he laughed until his sides shook.

"As much as Balin—as much as Baffin, his chief." And he added an old office joke, and laughed more than ever:

"It would not even do to send them by water to inspect the Point-du-Jour, for they would be sick on the penny steamboats on the Seine."

But she remained as serious as if she had not heard him, and then she said in a low voice, as she scratched her chin:

"If we only had a Deputy to fall back upon. When the Chamber hears everything that is going on at the Admiralty, the Minister will be turned out——"

She was interrupted by a terrible noise on the stairs. Marie-Louise and Philippe-Auguste, who had just come in from the gutter, were slapping each other all the way upstairs. Their mother rushed at them furiously, and taking each of them by an arm she dragged them into the room, shaking them vigorously; but as soon as they saw their father, they rushed up to him, and he kissed them affectionately, and taking one of them on each knee, began to talk to them.

Philippe-Auguste was an ugly, ill-kempt little brat, dirty from head to foot, with the face of an idiot, and Marie-Louise was already like her mother—spoke like her, repeated her words, and even imitated her movements. She also asked him whether there was anything fresh at the office, and he replied merrily:

"Your friend, Ramon, who comes and dines here every Sunday, is going to leave us, little one. There is a new second head-clerk."

She looked at her father, and with a precocious child's pity, she said:

"Another man has been put over your head again."

He stopped laughing, and did not reply, and in order to create a diversion, he said, addressing his wife, who was cleaning the windows:

"How is mamma, upstairs?"

Madame Caravan left off rubbing, turned round pulled her cap up, as it had fallen quite on to her back, and said with trembling lips:

"Ah! yes; let us talk about your mother, for she has made a pretty scene. Just imagine: a short time ago Madame Lebaudin, the hairdresser's wife, came upstairs to borrow a packet of starch of me, and, as I was not at home, your mother chased her out as though she were a beggar; but I gave it to the old woman. She pretended not to hear, as she always does when one tells her unpleasant truths, but she is no more deaf than I am, as you know. It is all a sham, and the proof of it is, that she went up to her own room immediately, without saying a word."

Caravan, embarrassed, did not utter a word, and at that moment the little servant came in to announce dinner. In order to let his mother know, he took a broom-handle, which always stood in a corner, and rapped loudly on the ceiling three times, and then they went into the dining-room. Madame Caravan, junior, helped the soup, and waited for the old woman, but she did not come, and as the soup was getting cold, they began to eat slowly, and when their plates were empty, they waited again, and Madame Caravan, who was furious, attacked her husband:

"She does it on purpose, you know that as well as I do. But you always uphold her."

Not knowing which side to take, he sent Marie-Louise to fetch her grandmother, and he sat motionless, with his eyes cast down, while his wife tapped her glass angrily with her knife. In about a minute, the door flew open suddenly, and the child came in again, out of breath and very pale, and said hurriedly:

"Grandmamma has fallen on the floor."

Caravan jumped up, threw his table-napkin down, and rushed upstairs, while his wife, who thought it was some trick of her mother-in-law's, followed more slowly, shrugging her shoulders, as if to express her doubt. When they got upstairs, however, they found the old woman lying at full length in the middle of the room; and when they turned her over, they saw that she was insensible and motionless, while her skin looked more wrinkled and yellow than usual, her eyes were closed, her teeth clenched, and her thin body was stiff.

Caravan knelt down by her, and began to moan.

"My poor mother! my poor mother!" he said. But the other Madame Caravan said:

"Bah! She has only fainted again, that is all, and she has done it to prevent us from dining comfortably, you may be sure of that."

They put her on the bed, undressed her completely, and Caravan, his wife, and the servant began to rub her; but, in spite of their efforts, she did not recover consciousness, so they sent Rosalie, the servant, to fetch Doctor Chenet. He lived a long way off, on the quay, going towards Suresnes, and so it was a considerable time before he arrived. He came at last, however, and, after having looked at the old woman, felt her pulse, and listened for a heart beat, he said: "It is all over."

Caravan threw himself on the body, sobbing violently; he kissed his mother's rigid face, and wept so that great tears fell on the dead woman's face like drops of water, and, naturally, Madame Caravan, junior, showed a decorous amount of grief, and uttered feeble moans as she stood behind her husband, while she rubbed her eyes vigorously.

But, suddenly, Caravan raised himself up, with his thin hair in disorder, and, looking very ugly in his grief, said:

"But—are you sure, doctor? Are you quite sure?"

The doctor stooped over the body, and, handling it with professional dexterity, as a shopkeeper might do, when showing off his goods, he said:

"See, my dear friend, look at her eye."

He raised the eyelid, and the old woman's eye appeared altogether unaltered, unless, perhaps, the pupil was rather larger, and Caravan felt a severe shock at the sight. Then Monsieur Chenet took her thin arm, forced the fingers open, and said, angrily, as if he had been contradicted:

"Just look at her hand; I never make a mistake, you may be quite sure of that."

Caravan fell on the bed, and almost bellowed, while his wife, still whimpering, did what was necessary.

She brought the night-table, on which she spread a towel and placed four wax candles on it, which she lighted; then she took a sprig of box, which was hanging over the chimney glass, and put it between the four candles, in a plate, which she filled with clean water, as she had no holy water. But, after a moment's rapid reflection, she threw a pinch of salt into the water, no doubt thinking she was performing some sort of act of consecration by doing that, and when she had finished, she remained standing motionless, and the doctor, who had been helping her, whispered to her:

"We must take Caravan away."

She nodded assent, and, going up to her husband, who was still on his knees, sobbing, she raised him up by one arm, while Chenet took him by the other.

They put him into a chair, and his wife kissed his forehead, and then began to lecture him. Chenet enforced her words and preached firmness, courage, and resignation—the very things which are always wanting in such overwhelming misfortunes—and then both of them took him by the arms again and led him out.

He was crying like a great child, with convulsive sobs; his arms hanging down, and his legs weak, and he went downstairs without knowing what he was doing, and moving his feet mechanically. They put him into the chair which he always occupied at dinner, in front of his empty soup plate. And there he sat, without moving, his eyes fixed on his glass, and so stupefied with grief, that he could not even think.

In a corner, Madame Caravan was talking with the doctor and asking what the necessary formalities were, as she wanted to obtain practical information. At last, Monsieur Chenet, who appeared to be waiting for something, took up his hat and prepared to go, saying that he had not dined yet; whereupon she exclaimed:

"What! you have not dined? Why, stay here, doctor; don't go. You shall have whatever we have, for, of course, you understand that we do not fare sumptuously." He made excuses and refused, but she persisted, and said: "You really must stay; at times like this, people like to have friends near them, and, besides that, perhaps you will be able to persuade my husband to take some nourishment; he must keep up his strength."

The doctor bowed, and, putting down his hat, he said:

"In that case, I will accept your invitation, madame."

She gave Rosalie, who seemed to have lost her head, some orders, and then sat down, "to pretend to eat," as she said, "to keep the doctor company."

The soup was brought in again, and Monsieur Chenet took two helpings. Then there came a dish of tripe, which exhaled a smell of onions, and which Madame Caravan made up her mind to taste.

"It is excellent," the doctor said, at which she smiled, and, turning to her husband, she said:

"Do take a little, my poor Alfred, only just to put something in your stomach. Remember that you have got to pass the night watching by her!"

He held out his plate, docilely, just as he would have gone to bed, if he had been told to, obeying her in everything, without resistance and without reflection, and he ate; the doctor helped himself three times, while Madame Caravan, from time to time, fished out a large piece at the end of her fork, and swallowed it with a sort of studied indifference.

When a salad bowl full of macaroni was brought in, the doctor said:

"By Jove! That is what I am very fond of." And this time, Madame Caravan helped everybody. She even filled the saucers that were being scraped by the children, who, being left to themselves, had been drinking wine without any water, and were now kicking each other under the table.

Chenet remembered that Rossini, the composer, had been very fond of that Italian dish, and suddenly he exclaimed:

"Why! that rhymes, and one could begin some lines like this:
    The Maestro Rossini
    Was fond of macaroni."

Nobody listened to him, however. Madame Caravan, who had suddenly grown thoughtful, was thinking of all the probable consequences of the event, while her husband made bread pellets, which he put on the table-cloth, and looked at with a fixed, idiotic stare. As he was devoured by thirst, he was continually raising his glass full of wine to his lips, and the consequence was that his mind, which had been upset by the shock and grief, seemed to become vague, and his ideas danced about as digestion commenced.

The doctor, who, meanwhile, had been drinking away steadily, was getting visibly drunk, and Madame Caravan herself felt the reaction which follows all nervous shocks, and was agitated and excited, and, although she had drunk nothing but water, her head felt rather confused.

Presently, Chenet began to relate stories of death that appeared comical to him. For in that suburb of Paris, that is full of people from the provinces, one finds that indifference towards death which all peasants show, were it even their own father or mother; that want of respect, that unconscious brutality which is so common in the country, and so rare in Paris, and he said:

"Why, I was sent for last week to the Rue du Puteaux, and when

I went, I found the patient dead and the whole family calmly sitting beside the bed finishing a bottle of aniseed cordial, which had been bought the night before to satisfy the dying man's fancy."

But Madame Caravan was not listening; she was continually thinking of the inheritance, and Caravan was incapable of understanding anything further.

Coffee was presently served, and it had been made very strong to give them courage. As every cup was well flavored with cognac, it made all their faces red, and confused their ideas still more. To make matters still worse, Chenet suddenly seized the brandy bottle and poured out "a drop for each of them just to wash their mouths out with," as he termed it, and then, without speaking any more, overcome in spite of themselves, by that feeling of animal comfort which alcohol affords after dinner, they slowly sipped the sweet cognac, which formed a yellowish syrup at the bottom of their cups.

The children had fallen asleep, and Rosalie carried them off to bed. Caravan, mechanically obeying that wish to forget oneself which possesses all unhappy persons, helped himself to brandy again several times, and his dull eyes grew bright. At last the doctor rose to go, and seizing his friend's arm, he said:

"Come with me; a little fresh air will do you good. When one is in trouble, one must not remain in one spot."

The other obeyed mechanically, put on his hat, took his stick, and went out, and both of them walked arm-in-arm towards the Seine, in the starlight night.

The air was warm and sweet, for all the gardens in the neighborhood were full of flowers at this season of the year, and their fragrance, which is scarcely perceptible during the day, seemed to awaken at the approach of night, and mingled with the light breezes which blew upon them in the darkness.

The broad avenue with its two rows of gas lamps, that extended as far as the Arc de Triomphe, was deserted and silent, but there was the distant roar of Paris, which seemed to have a reddish vapor hanging over it. It was a kind of continual rumbling, which was at times answered by the whistle of a train in the distance, travelling at full speed to the ocean, through the provinces.

The fresh air on the faces of the two men rather overcame them at first, made the doctor lose his equilibrium a little, and increased Caravan's giddiness, from which he had suffered since dinner. He walked as if he were in a dream; his thoughts were paralyzed, although he felt no great grief, for he was in a state of mental torpor that prevented him from suffering, and he even felt a sense of relief which was increased by the mildness of the night.

When they reached the bridge, they turned to the right, and got the fresh breeze from the river, which rolled along, calm and melancholy, bordered by tall poplar trees, while the stars looked as if they were floating on the water and were moving with the current. A slight white mist that floated over the opposite banks, filled their lungs with a sensation of cold, and Caravan stopped suddenly, for he was struck by that smell from the water which brought back old memories to his mind. For, in his mind, he suddenly saw his mother again, in Picardy, as he had seen her years before, kneeling in front of their door, and washing the heaps of linen at her side in the stream that ran through their garden. He almost fancied that he could hear the sound of the wooden paddle with which she beat the linen in the calm silence of the country, and her voice, as she called out to him: "Alfred, bring me some soap." And he smelled that odor of running water, of the mist rising from the wet ground, that marshy smell, which he should never forget, and which came back to him on this very evening on which his mother had died.

He stopped, seized with a feeling of despair. A sudden flash seemed to reveal to him the extent of his calamity, and that breath from the river plunged him into an abyss of hopeless grief. His life seemed cut in half, his youth disappeared, swallowed up by that death. All the former days were over and done with, all the recollections of his youth had been swept away; for the future, there would be nobody to talk to him of what had happened in days gone by, of the people he had known of old, of his own part of the country, and of his past life; that was a part of his existence which existed no longer, and the rest might as well end now.

And then he saw "the mother" as she was when young, wearing well-worn dresses, which he remembered for such a long time that they seemed inseparable from her; he recollected her movements, the different tones of her voice, her habits, her predilections, her fits of anger, the wrinkles on her face, the movements of her thin fingers, and all her well-known attitudes, which she would never have again, and clutching hold of the doctor, he began to moan and weep. His thin legs began to tremble, his whole stout body was shaken by his sobs, all he could say was:

"My mother, my poor mother, my poor mother!"

But his companion, who was still drunk, and who intended to finish the evening in certain places of bad repute that he frequented secretly, made him sit down on the grass by the riverside, and left him almost immediately, under the pretext that he had to see a patient.

Caravan went on crying for some time, and when he had got to the end of his tears, when his grief had, so to say, run out, he again felt relief, repose and sudden tranquillity.

The moon had risen, and bathed the horizon in its soft light.

The tall poplar trees had a silvery sheen on them, and the mist on the plain looked like drifting snow; the river, in which the stars were reflected, and which had a sheen as of mother-of-pearl, was gently rippled by the wind. The air was soft and sweet, and Caravan inhaled it almost greedily, and thought that he could perceive a feeling of freshness, of calm and of superhuman consolation pervading him.

He actually resisted that feeling of comfort and relief, and kept on saying to himself: "My poor mother, my poor mother!" and tried to make himself cry, from a kind of conscientious feeling; but he could not succeed in doing so any longer, and those sad thoughts, which had made him sob so bitterly a shore time before, had almost passed away. In a few moments, he rose to go home, and returned slowly, under the influence of that serene night, and with a heart soothed in spite of himself.

When he reached the bridge, he saw that the last tramcar was ready to start, and behind it were the brightly lighted windows of the Cafe du Globe. He felt a longing to tell somebody of his loss, to excite pity, to make himself interesting. He put on a woeful face, pushed open the door, and went up to the counter, where the landlord still was. He had counted on creating a sensation, and had hoped that everybody would get up and come to him with outstretched hands, and say: "Why, what is the matter with you?" But nobody noticed his disconsolate face, so he rested his two elbows on the counter, and, burying his face in his hands, he murmured: "Mon Dieu! Mon Dieu!"

The landlord looked at him and said: "Are you ill, Monsieur Caravan?"

"No, my friend," he replied, "but my mother has just died."

"Ah!" the other exclaimed, and as a customer at the other end of the establishment asked for a glass of Bavarian beer, he went to attend to him, leaving Caravan dumfounded at his want of sympathy.

The three domino players were sitting at the same table which they had occupied before dinner, totally absorbed in their game, and Caravan went up to them, in search of pity, but as none of them appeared to notice him he made up his mind to speak.

"A great misfortune has happened to me since I was here," he said.

All three slightly raised their heads at the same instant, but keeping their eyes fixed on the pieces which they held in their hands.

"What do you say?"

"My mother has just died"; whereupon one of them said:

"Oh! the devil," with that false air of sorrow which indifferent people assume. Another, who could not find anything to say, emitted a sort of sympathetic whistle, shaking his head at the same time, and the third turned to the game again, as if he were saying to himself: "Is that all!"

Caravan had expected some of these expressions that are said to "come from the heart," and when he saw how his news was received, he left the table, indignant at their calmness at their friend's sorrow, although this sorrow had stupefied him so that he scarcely felt it any longer. When he got home his wife was waiting for him in her nightgown, and sitting in a low chair by the open window, still thinking of the inheritance.

"Undress yourself," she said; "we can go on talking."

He raised his head, and looking at the ceiling, said:

"But—there is nobody upstairs."

"I beg your pardon, Rosalie is with her, and you can go and take her place at three o'clock in the morning, when you have had some sleep."

He only partially undressed, however, so as to be ready for anything that might happen, and after tying a silk handkerchief round his head, he lay down to rest, and for some time neither of them spoke. Madame Caravan was thinking.

Her nightcap was adorned with a red bow, and was pushed rather to one side, as was the way with all the caps she wore, and presently she turned towards him and said:

"Do you know whether your mother made a will?"

He hesitated for a moment, and then replied:

"I—I do not think so. No, I am sure that she did not."

His wife looked at him, and she said, in a low, angry tone:

"I call that infamous; here we have been wearing ourselves out for ten years in looking after her, and have boarded and lodged her! Your sister would not have done so much for her, nor I either, if I had known how I was to be rewarded! Yes, it is a disgrace to her memory! I dare say that you will tell me that she paid us, but one cannot pay one's children in ready money for what they do; that obligation is recognized after death; at any rate, that is how honorable people act. So I have had all my worry and trouble for nothing! Oh, that is nice! that is very nice!"

Poor Caravan, who was almost distracted, kept on repeating:

"My dear, my dear, please, please be quiet."

She grew calmer by degrees, and, resuming her usual voice and manner, she continued:

"We must let your sister know to-morrow."

He started, and said:

"Of course we must; I had forgotten all about it; I will send her a telegram the first thing in the morning."

"No," she replied, like a woman who had foreseen everything; "no, do not send it before ten or eleven o'clock, so that we may have time to turn round before she comes. It does not take more than two hours to get here from Charenton, and we can say that you lost your head from grief. If we let her know in the course of the day, that will be soon enough, and will give us time to look round."

Caravan put his hand to his forehead, and, in the came timid voice in which he always spoke of his chief, the very thought of whom made him tremble, he said:

"I must let them know at the office."

"Why?" she replied. "On occasions like this, it is always excusable to forget. Take my advice, and don't let him know; your chief will not be able to say anything to you, and you will put him in a nice fix.

"Oh! yes, that I shall, and he will be in a terrible rage, too, when he notices my absence. Yes, you are right; it is a capital idea, and when I tell him that my mother is dead, he will be obliged to hold his tongue."

And he rubbed his hands in delight at the joke, when he thought of his chief's face; while upstairs lay the body of the dead old woman, with the servant asleep beside it.

But Madame Caravan grew thoughtful, as if she were preoccupied by something which she did not care to mention, and at last she said:

"Your mother had given you her clock, had she not—the girl playing at cup and ball?"

He thought for a moment, and then replied:

"Yes, yes; she said to me (but it was a long time ago, when she first came here): 'I shall leave the clock to you, if you look after me well.'"

Madame Caravan was reassured, and regained her serenity, and said:

"Well, then, you must go and fetch it out of her room, for if we get your sister here, she will prevent us from taking it."

He hesitated.

"Do you think so?"

That made her angry.

"I certainly think so; once it is in our possession, she will know nothing at all about where it came from; it belongs to us. It is just the same with the chest of drawers with the marble top, that is in her room; she gave it me one day when she was in a good temper. We will bring it down at the same time."

Caravan, however, seemed incredulous, and said:

"But, my dear, it is a great responsibility!"

She turned on him furiously.

"Oh! Indeed! Will you never change? You would let your children die of hunger, rather than make a move. Does not that chest of drawers belong to us, as she gave it to me? And if your sister is not satisfied, let her tell me so, me! I don't care a straw for your sister. Come, get up, and we will bring down what your mother gave us, immediately."

Trembling and vanquished, he got out of bed and began to put on his trousers, but she stopped him:

"It is not worth while to dress yourself; your underwear is quite enough. I mean to go as I am."

They both left the room in their night clothes, went upstairs quite noiselessly, opened the door and went into the room, where the four lighted tapers and the plate with the sprig of box alone seemed to be watching the old woman in her rigid repose, for Rosalie, who was lying back in the easy chair with her legs stretched out, her hands folded in her lap, and her head on one side, was also quite motionless, and was snoring with her mouth wide open.

Caravan took the clock, which was one of those grotesque objects that were produced so plentifully under the Empire. A girl in gilt bronze was holding a cup and ball, and the ball formed the pendulum.

"Give that to me," his wife said, "and take the marble slab off the chest of drawers."

He put the marble slab on his shoulder with considerable effort, and they left the room. Caravan had to stoop in the doorway, and trembled as he went downstairs, while his wife walked backwards, so as to light him, and held the candlestick in one hand, carrying the clock under the other arm.

When they were in their own room, she heaved a sigh.

"We have got over the worst part of the job," she said; "so now let us go and fetch the other things."

But the bureau drawers were full of the old woman's wearing apparel, which they must manage to hide somewhere, and Madame Caravan soon thought of a plan.

"Go and get that wooden packing case in the vestibule; it is hardly worth anything, and we may just as well put it here."

And when he had brought it upstairs they began to fill it. One by one they took out all the collars, cuffs, chemises, caps, all the well-worn things that had belonged to the poor woman lying there behind them, and arranged them methodically in the wooden box in such a manner as to deceive Madame Braux, the deceased woman's other child, who would be coming the next day.

When they had finished, they first of all carried the bureau drawers downstairs, and the remaining portion afterwards, each of them holding an end, and it was some time before they could make up their minds where it would stand best; but at last they decided upon their own room, opposite the bed, between the two windows, and as soon as it was in its place Madame Caravan filled it with her own things. The clock was placed on the chimney-piece in the dining-room, and they looked to see what the effect was, and were both delighted with it and agreed that nothing could be better. Then they retired, she blew out the candle, and soon everybody in the house was asleep.

It was broad daylight when. Caravan opened his eyes again. His mind was rather confused when he woke up, and he did not clearly remember what had happened for a few minutes; when he did, he felt a weight at his heart, and jumped out of bed, almost ready to cry again.

He hastened to the room overhead, where Rosalie was still sleeping in the same position as the night before, not having awakened once. He sent her to do her work, put fresh tapers in the place of those that had burnt out, and then he looked at his mother, revolving in his brain those apparently profound thoughts, those religious and philosophical commonplaces which trouble people of mediocre intelligence in the presence of death.

But, as his wife was calling him, he went downstairs. She had written out a list of what had to be done during the morning, and he was horrified when he saw the memorandum:

1. Report the death at the mayor's office. 2. See the doctor who had attended her. 3. Order the coffin. 4. Give notice at the church. 5. Go to the undertaker. 6. Order the notices of her death at the printer's. 7. Go to the lawyer. 8. Telegraph the news to all the family.

Besides all this, there were a number of small commissions; so he took his hat and went out. As the news had spread abroad, Madame Caravan's female friends and neighbors soon began to come in and begged to be allowed to see the body. There had been a scene between husband and wife at the hairdresser's on the ground floor about the matter, while a customer was being shaved. The wife, who was knitting steadily, said: "Well, there is one less, and as great a miser as one ever meets with. I certainly did not care for her; but, nevertheless, I must go and have a look at her."

The husband, while lathering his patient's chin, said: "That is another queer fancy! Nobody but a woman would think of such a thing. It is not enough for them to worry you during life, but they cannot even leave you at peace when you are dead:" But his wife, without being in the least disconcerted, replied: "The feeling is stronger than I am, and I must go. It has been on me since the morning. If I were not to see her, I should think about it all my life; but when I have had a good look at her, I shall be satisfied."

The knight of the razor shrugged his shoulders and remarked in a low voice to the gentleman whose cheek he was scraping: "I just ask you, what sort of ideas do you think these confounded females have? I should not amuse myself by going to see a corpse!" But his wife had heard him and replied very quietly: "But it is so, it is so." And then, putting her knitting on the counter, she went upstairs to the first floor, where she met two other neighbors, who had just come, and who were discussing the event with Madame Caravan, who was giving them the details, and they all went together to the death chamber. The four women went in softly, and, one after the other, sprinkled the bed clothes with the salt water, knelt down, made the sign of the cross while they mumbled a prayer. Then they rose from their knees and looked for some time at the corpse with round, wide-open eyes and mouths partly open, while the daughter-in-law of the dead woman, with her handkerchief to her face, pretended to be sobbing piteously.

When she turned about to walk away whom should she perceive standing close to the door but Marie-Louise and Philippe-Auguste, who were curiously taking stock of all that was going on. Then, forgetting her pretended grief, she threw herself upon them with uplifted hands, crying out in a furious voice, "Will you get out of this, you horrid brats!"

Ten minutes later, going upstairs again with another contingent of neighbors, she prayed, wept profusely, performed all her duties, and found once more her two children, who had followed her upstairs. She again boxed their ears soundly, but the next time she paid no heed to them, and at each fresh arrival of visitors the two urchins always followed in the wake, kneeling down in a corner and imitating slavishly everything they saw their mother do.

When the afternoon came the crowds of inquisitive people began to diminish, and soon there were no more visitors. Madame Caravan, returning to her own apartments, began to make the necessary preparations for the funeral ceremony, and the deceased was left alone.

The window of the room was open. A torrid heat entered, along with clouds of dust; the flames of the four candles were flickering beside the immobile corpse, and upon the cloth which covered the face, the closed eyes, the two stretched-out hands, small flies alighted, came, went and careered up and down incessantly, being the only companions of the old woman for the time being.

Marie-Louise and Philippe-Auguste, however, had now left the house and were running up and down the street. They were soon surrounded by their playmates, by little girls especially, who were older and who were much more interested in all the mysteries of life, asking questions as if they were grown people.

"Then your grandmother is dead?" "Yes, she died yesterday evening." "What does a dead person look like?"

Then Marie began to explain, telling all about the candles, the sprig of box and the face of the corpse. It was not long before great curiosity was aroused in the minds of all the children, and they asked to be allowed to go upstairs to look at the departed.

Marie-Louise at once organized a first expedition, consisting of five girls and two boys—the biggest and the most courageous. She made them take off their shoes so that they might not be discovered. The troupe filed into the house and mounted the stairs as stealthily as an army of mice.

Once in the chamber, the little girl, imitating her mother, regulated the ceremony. She solemnly walked in advance of her comrades, went down on her knees, made the sign of the cross, moved her lips as in prayer, rose, sprinkled the bed, and while the children, all crowded together, were approaching—frightened and curious and eager to look at the face and hands of the deceased—she began suddenly to simulate sobbing and to bury her eyes in her little handkerchief. Then, becoming instantly consoled, on thinking of the other children who were downstairs waiting at the door, she ran downstairs followed by the rest, returning in a minute with another group, then a third; for all the little ragamuffins of the countryside, even to the little beggars in rags, had congregated in order to participate in this new pleasure; and each time she repeated her mother's grimaces with absolute perfection.

At length, however, she became tired. Some game or other drew the children away from the house, and the old grandmother was left alone, forgotten suddenly by everybody.

The room was growing dark, and upon the dry and rigid features of the corpse the fitful flames of the candles cast patches of light.

Towards 8 o'clock Caravan ascended to the chamber of death, closed the windows and renewed the candles. He was now quite composed on entering the room, accustomed already to regard the corpse as though it had been there for months. He even went the length of declaring that, as yet, there were no signs of decomposition, making this remark just at the moment when he and his wife were about to sit down at table. "Pshaw!" she responded, "she is now stark and stiff; she will keep for a year."

The soup was eaten in silence. The children, who had been left to themselves all day, now worn out by fatigue, were sleeping soundly on their chairs, and nobody ventured to break the silence.

Suddenly the flame of the lamp went down. Madame Caravan immediately turned up the wick, a hollow sound ensued, and the light went out. They had forgotten to buy oil. To send for it now to the grocer's would keep back the dinner, and they began to look for candles, but none were to be found except the tapers which had been placed upon the table upstairs in the death chamber.

Madame Caravan, always prompt in her decisions, quickly despatched Marie-Louise to fetch two, and her return was awaited in total darkness.

The footsteps of the girl who had ascended the stairs were distinctly heard. There was silence for a few seconds and then the child descended precipitately. She threw open the door and in a choking voice murmured: "Oh! papa, grandmamma is dressing herself!"

Caravan bounded to his feet with such precipitance that his chair fell over against the wall. He stammered out: "You say? . . . . What are you saying?"

But Marie-Louise, gasping with emotion, repeated: "Grand— grand —grandmamma is putting on her clothes, she is coming downstairs."

Caravan rushed boldly up the staircase, followed by his wife, dumfounded; but he came to a standstill before the door of the second floor, overcome with terror, not daring to enter. What was he going to see? Madame Caravan, more courageous, turned the handle of the door and stepped forward into the room.

The old woman was standing up. In awakening from her lethargic sleep, before even regaining full consciousness, in turning upon her side and raising herself on her elbow, she had extinguished three of the candles which burned near the bed. Then, gaining strength, she got off the bed and began to look for her clothes. The absence of her chest of drawers had at first worried her, but, after a little, she had succeeded in finding her things at the bottom of the wooden box, and was now quietly dressing. She emptied the plateful of water, replaced the sprig of box behind the looking-glass, and arranged the chairs in their places, and was ready to go downstairs when there appeared before her her son and daughter-in-law.

Caravan rushed forward, seized her by the hands, embraced her with tears in his eyes, while his wife, who was behind him, repeated in a hypocritical tone of voice: "Oh, what a blessing! oh, what a blessing!"

But the old woman, without being at all moved, without even appearing to understand, rigid as a statue, and with glazed eyes, simply asked: "Will dinner soon be ready?"

He stammered out, not knowing what he said:

"Oh, yes, mother, we have been waiting for you."

And with an alacrity unusual in him, he took her arm, while Madame Caravan, the younger, seized the candle and lighted them downstairs, walking backwards in front of them, step by step, just as she had done the previous night for her husband, who was carrying the marble.

On reaching the first floor, she almost ran against people who were ascending the stairs. It was the Charenton family, Madame Braux, followed by her husband.

The wife, tall and stout, with a prominent stomach, opened wide her terrified eyes and was ready to make her escape. The husband, a socialist shoemaker, a little hairy man, the perfect image of a monkey, murmured quite unconcerned: "Well, what next? Is she resurrected?"

As soon as Madame Caravan recognized them, she made frantic gestures to them; then, speaking aloud, she said: "Why, here you are! What a pleasant surprise!"

But Madame Braux, dumfounded, understood nothing. She responded in a low voice: "It was your telegram that brought us; we thought that all was over."

Her husband, who was behind her, pinched her to make her

keep silent. He added with a sly laugh, which his thick beard concealed: "It was very kind of you to invite us here. We set out post haste," which remark showed the hostility which had for a long time reigned between the households. Then, just as the old woman reached the last steps, he pushed forward quickly and rubbed his hairy face against her cheeks, shouting in her ear, on account of her deafness: "How well you look, mother; sturdy as usual, hey!"

Madame Braux, in her stupefaction at seeing the old woman alive, whom they all believed to be dead, dared not even embrace her; and her enormous bulk blocked up the passageway and hindered the others from advancing. The old woman, uneasy and suspicious, but without speaking, looked at everyone around her; and her little gray eyes, piercing and hard, fixed themselves now on one and now on the other, and they were so full of meaning that the children became frightened.

Caravan, to explain matters, said: "She has been somewhat ill, but she is better now; quite well, indeed, are you not, mother?"

Then the good woman, continuing to walk, replied in a husky voice, as though it came from a distance: "It was syncope. I heard you all the while."

An embarrassing silence followed. They entered the dining-room, and in a few minutes all sat down to an improvised dinner.

Only M. Braux had retained his self-possession. His gorilla features grinned wickedly, while he let fall some words of double meaning which painfully disconcerted everyone.

But the door bell kept ringing every second, and Rosalie, distracted, came to call Caravan, who rushed out, throwing down his napkin. His brother-in-law even asked him whether it was not one of his reception days, to which he stammered out in answer: "No, only a few packages; nothing more."

A parcel was brought in, which he began to open carelessly, and the mourning announcements with black borders appeared unexpectedly. Reddening up to the very eyes, he closed the package hurriedly and pushed it under his waistcoat.

His mother had not seen it! She was looking intently at her clock which stood on the mantelpiece, and the embarrassment increased in midst of a dead silence. Turning her wrinkled face towards her daughter, the old woman, in whose eyes gleamed malice, said: "On Monday you must take me away from here, so that I can see your little girl. I want so much to see her." Madame Braux, her features all beaming, exclaimed: "Yes, mother, that

I will," while Madame Caravan, the younger, who had turned pale, was ready to faint with annoyance. The two men, however, gradually drifted into conversation and soon became embroiled in a political discussion. Braux maintained the most revolutionary and communistic doctrines, his eyes glowing, and gesticulating and throwing about his arms. "Property, sir," he said, "is a robbery perpetrated on the working classes; the land is the common property of every man; hereditary rights are an infamy and a disgrace." But here he suddenly stopped, looking as if he had just said something foolish, then added in softer tones: "But this is not the proper moment to discuss such things."

The door was opened and Dr. Chenet appeared. For a moment he seemed bewildered, but regaining his usual smirking expression of countenance, he jauntily approached the old woman and said: "Aha! mamma; you are better to-day. Oh! I never had any doubt but you would come round again; in fact, I said to myself as I was mounting the staircase, 'I have an idea that I shall find the old lady on her feet once more';" and as he patted her gently on the back: "Ah! she is as solid as the Pont-Neuf, she will bury us all; see if she does not."

He sat down, accepted the coffee that was offered him, and soon began to join in the conversation of the two men, backing up Braux, for he himself had been mixed up in the Commune.

The old woman, now feeling herself fatigued, wished to retire. Caravan rushed forward. She looked him steadily in the eye and said: "You, you must carry my clock and chest of drawers upstairs again without a moment's delay." "Yes, mamma," he replied, gasping; "yes, I will do so." The old woman then took the arm of her daughter and withdrew from the room. The two Caravans remained astounded, silent, plunged in the deepest despair, while Braux rubbed his hands and sipped his coffee gleefully.

Suddenly Madame Caravan, consumed with rage, rushed at him, exclaiming: "You are a thief, a footpad, a cur! I would spit in your face! I—I —would——" She could find nothing further to say, suffocating as she was with rage, while he went on sipping his coffee with a smile.

His wife returning just then, Madame Caravan attacked her sister-in-law, and the two women—the one with her enormous bulk, the other epileptic and spare, with changed voices and trembling hands flew at one another with words of abuse.

Chenet and Braux now interposed, and the latter, taking his better half by the shoulders, pushed her out of the door before him, shouting: "Go on, you slut; you talk too much"; and the two were heard in the street quarrelling until they disappeared from sight.

M. Chenet also took his departure, leaving the Caravans alone, face to face. The husband fell back on his chair, and with the cold sweat standing out in beads on his temples, murmured: "What shall I say to my chief to-morrow?"

BESIDE SCHOPENHAUER'S CORPSE

He was slowly dying, as consumptives die. I saw him each day, about two o'clock, sitting beneath the hotel windows on a bench in the promenade, looking out on the calm sea. He remained for some time without moving, in the heat of the sun, gazing mournfully at the Mediterranean. Every now and then, he cast a glance at the lofty mountains with beclouded summits that shut in Mentone; then, with a very slow movement, he would cross his long legs, so thin that they seemed like two bones, around which fluttered the cloth of his trousers, and he would open a book, always the same book. And then he did not stir any more, but read on, read on with his eye and his mind; all his wasting body seemed to read, all his soul plunged, lost, disappeared, in this book, up to the hour when the cool air made him cough a little. Then, he got up and reentered the hotel.

He was a tall German, with fair beard, who breakfasted and dined in his own room, and spoke to nobody.

A vague, curiosity attracted me to him. One day, I sat down by his side, having taken up a book, too, to keep up appearances, a volume of Musset's poems.

And I began to look through "Rolla."

Suddenly, my neighbor said to me, in good French:

"Do you know German, monsieur?"

"Not at all, monsieur."

"I am sorry for that. Since chance has thrown us side by side, I could have lent you, I could have shown you, an inestimable thing—this book which I hold in my hand."

"What is it, pray?"

"It is a copy of my master, Schopenhauer, annotated with his own hand. All the margins, as you may see, are covered with his handwriting."

I took the book from him reverently, and I gazed at these forms incomprehensible to me, but which revealed the immortal thoughts of the greatest shatterer of dreams who had ever dwelt on earth.

And Musset's verses arose in my memory:
  "Hast thou found out, Voltaire, that it is bliss to die,
  And does thy hideous smile over thy bleached bones fly?"

And involuntarily I compared the childish sarcasm, the religious sarcasm of Voltaire with the irresistible irony of the German philosopher whose influence is henceforth ineffaceable.

Let us protest and let us be angry, let us be indignant, or let us be enthusiastic, Schopenhauer has marked humanity with the seal of his disdain and of his disenchantment.

A disabused pleasure-seeker, he overthrew beliefs, hopes, poetic ideals and chimeras, destroyed the aspirations, ravaged the confidence of souls, killed love, dragged down the chivalrous worship of women, crushed the illusions of hearts, and accomplished the most gigantic task ever attempted by scepticism. He spared nothing with his mocking spirit, and exhausted everything. And even to-day those who execrate him seem to carry in their own souls particles of his thought.

"So, then, you were intimately acquainted with Schopenhauer?" I said to the German.

He smiled sadly.

"Up to the time of his death, monsieur."

And he spoke to me about the philosopher and told me about the almost supernatural impression which this strange being made on all who came near him.

He gave me an account of the interview of the old iconoclast with a French politician, a doctrinaire Republican, who wanted to get a glimpse of this man, and found him in a noisy tavern, seated in the midst of his disciples, dry, wrinkled, laughing with an unforgettable laugh, attacking and tearing to pieces ideas and beliefs with a single word, as a dog tears with one bite of his teeth the tissues with which he plays.

He repeated for me the comment of this Frenchman as he went away, astonished and terrified: "I thought I had spent an hour with the devil."

Then he added:

"He had, indeed, monsieur, a frightful smile, which terrified us even after his death. I can tell you an anecdote about it that is not generally known, if it would interest you."

And he began, in a languid voice, interrupted by frequent fits of coughing.

"Schopenhauer had just died, and it was arranged that we should watch, in turn, two by two, till morning.

"He was lying in a large apartment, very simple, vast and gloomy. Two wax candles were burning on the stand by the bedside.

"It was midnight when I went on watch, together with one of our comrades. The two friends whom we replaced had left the apartment, and we came and sat down at the foot of the bed.

"The face was not changed. It was laughing. That pucker which we knew so well lingered still around the corners of the lips, and it seemed to us that he was about to open his eyes, to move and to speak. His thought, or rather his thoughts, enveloped us. We felt ourselves more than ever in the atmosphere of his genius, absorbed, possessed by him. His domination seemed to be even more sovereign now that he was dead. A feeling of mystery was blended with the power of this incomparable spirit.

"The bodies of these men disappear, but they themselves remain; and in the night which follows the cessation of their heart's pulsation I assure you, monsieur, they are terrifying.

"And in hushed tones we talked about him, recalling to mind certain sayings, certain formulas of his, those startling maxims which are like jets of flame flung, in a few words, into the darkness of the Unknown Life.

"'It seems to me that he is going to speak,' said my comrade. And we stared with uneasiness bordering on fear at the motionless face, with its eternal laugh. Gradually, we began to feel ill at ease, oppressed, on the point of fainting. I faltered:

"'I don't know what is the matter with me, but, I assure you I am not well.'

"And at that moment we noticed that there was an unpleasant odor from the corpse.

"Then, my comrade suggested that we should go into the adjoining room, and leave the door open; and I assented to his proposal.

"I took one of the wax candles which burned on the stand, and I left the second behind. Then we went and sat down at the other end of the adjoining apartment, in such a position that we could see the bed and the corpse, clearly revealed by the light.

"But he still held possession of us. One would have said that his immaterial essence, liberated, free, all-powerful and dominating, was flitting around us. And sometimes, too, the dreadful odor of the decomposed body came toward us and penetrated us, sickening and indefinable.

"Suddenly a shiver passed through our bones: a sound, a slight sound, came from the death-chamber. Immediately we fixed our glances on him, and we saw, yes, monsieur, we saw distinctly, both of us, something white pass across the bed, fall on the carpet, and vanish under an armchair.

"We were on our feet before we had time to think of anything, distracted by stupefying terror, ready to run away. Then we stared at each other. We were horribly pale. Our hearts throbbed fiercely enough to have raised the clothing on our chests. I was the first to speak:

"'Did you see?'

"'Yes, I saw.'

"'Can it be that he is not dead?'

"'Why, when the body is putrefying?'

"'What are we to do?'

"My companion said in a hesitating tone:

"'We must go and look.'

"I took our wax candle and entered first, glancing into all the dark corners in the large apartment. Nothing was moving now, and I approached the bed. But I stood transfixed with stupor and fright:

"Schopenhauer was no longer laughing! He was grinning in a horrible fashion, with his lips pressed together and deep hollows in his cheeks. I stammered out:

"'He is not dead!'

"But the terrible odor ascended to my nose and stifled me. And I no longer moved, but kept staring fixedly at him, terrified as if in the presence of an apparition.

"Then my companion, having seized the other wax candle, bent forward. Next, he touched my arm without uttering a word. I followed his glance, and saw on the ground, under the armchair by the side of the bed, standing out white on the dark carpet, and open as if to bite, Schopenhauer's set of artificial teeth.

"The work of decomposition, loosening the jaws, had made it jump out of the mouth.

"I was really frightened that day, monsieur."

And as the sun was sinking toward the glittering sea, the consumptive German rose from his seat, gave me a parting bow, and retired into the hotel.

CPSIA information can be obtained
at www.ICGtesting.com
Printed in the USA
LVHW091356160720
660698LV00043B/667

9 781641 817400